HELLO THE UNKNOWN

HELLO THE UNKNOWN

Sandrine Marlier-Riquier

PEACEFUL DAILY, INC.

Library of Congress Control Number: 2015957385

Published by Peaceful Daily, Inc.
www.peacefuldaily.com

ISBN: 978-0-9970143-4-1
EISBN: 978-0-9970143-5-8

Book design by Perseus-Design.com
Cover art by: Tony Ceddia

Printed in the United States of America.

First Edition

10 9 8 7 6 5 4 3 2 1

PART I

Certainly, travel is more than the seeing of sights; it is a change that goes on, deep and permanent, in the ideas of living.

—Miriam Beard

Chapter 1

The streets are empty and the temple I came to visit in Phuket is quiet. We've been shooting on this tourist trap of an island for a week and I needed to find some peace this morning, far away from the seemingly endless supply of trinkets being plied on the swarms of foreigners that cluttered this part of Thailand. The humidity has made a mess of my hair, which will make the job of the hair and makeup artist that much more difficult when we start work later today. We have two more spreads left to photograph before we wrap this shoot. When I arrived at Wat Chalong, a few people had come for prayers. Palms touching, they held white lotus flowers and shook incense sticks in the air. I stared at the big golden Buddha for a long time. I wanted some guidance about my career and my relationship with Andrew, but I didn't know how to ask for it. I walked out with the same uneasy feelings I've had for months.

I have been waiting for a while for a taxi when a man in a khaki uniform marches past me.

"Sawade!" The officer doesn't answer my greeting. I follow him, hoping to make him stop. "Excuse me, Sir, any taxis come this way?" No response. I try again. "Taxi? Tuk-tuk?"

"Full Moon party," he answers.

Piles of garbage lie in front of the iron gates and a few tired locals sweep the streets with their straw brooms. It looks like it was quite a celebration. I have to get back to the hotel on time and will need a few minutes to freshen up before I start work. The lack of traffic and relative silence is unusual, considering how popular this place is. Plastic blue awnings flutter over the empty food stalls arranged in front of the golden temple, like secret witnesses to a holy ceremony.

A whistling sound pierces the air and the officer turns to me. "Motorbike ok?"

My client made me promise not to get on a bike, but I'm sure they'd rather have me back on time to finish the catalogue. The sky was so grey when we woke up that the photographer decided to wait and see if it would clear up. We all got the morning off. I had breakfast with Sarah, the other model, before she left for the airport to go back to New York. Another job was waiting for her in Alaska. I ask the driver if he has a helmet. He doesn't. At least I asked.

I hold on tight to the bike, both hands gripping the back handle bar. My arm muscles tense up, but the rest of my body, surprisingly, relaxes. A certain familiarity sweeps in. I remember putting my arms around Paul's waist five years ago and getting lost in Pai, a small town up north in Thailand. Together we rode past the murky river and misty waterfalls, up mountains and down hills. It was a year before the tsunami. (I never wanted to go back after the tragedy.) The wind gently brushes my face and I close my eyes. I never felt freer than on a motorbike with Paul. Sweet, happy memories from that year of backpacking wash over me: the old man growing cotton in his backyard, my scarf…

Being back in Thailand, I can't help thinking about Paul, expecting to see him at every street corner. Finding myself in the same place confuses me. It's as if I am reliving one love story while being inside another one. I moved in with Andrew last month, a decision I'm questioning. We've been dating for over two years but I'm not certain that we are right for each other.

The driver suddenly accelerates and I hold on tighter to the bike. We drive down the road that runs parallel to the beach, past several high-rise condos, American coffeehouses and mini-markets. I hear more German than Thai in the busy streets, which takes away almost all sense of the exotic and yet I smell frangipani flowers and incense, and freshly skinned chicken and spices.

When I arrive back at the hotel, the team is just sitting down to have lunch outside. The sky has cleared up, but the sun is too high now; we should be able to shoot in an hour. Being dependent on everyone else to be ready and every circumstance to be perfect for me to do my job can be challenging, and playing the monkey in bikini on a beach for a week straight is not as dreamy as I once thought it was. I much needed this morning break. I take a bowl of mango and sticky rice from the buffet table and go and sit on the beach.

Andrew has an important sales meeting today. I tap out a quick email on my phone to wish him good luck. I have another job in Miami next week, I type. I'm taking the money, as you say. I hate this expression, it sounds so mindless. I erase it. When we spend time together, I'll feel close to Andrew again, I reassure myself. During catalogue season, I only see Andrew for a day or two between shoots and I start to feel like we're strangers. I've been traveling a lot this past month, and already feel burnt out. I add, Let's plan a little trip, just you and me.

While I promised to quit smoking soon, Andrew has promised to come home to France with me for Christmas, and to learn some French. I need time with him before December though—just a few days. I've been looking at hotels in upstate New York. "Love you," I tap out. I sit down on the steps of the hotel restaurant and light a cigarette that tastes a little sweet and spicy. It is the usual brand I smoke, but I bought this pack at the local airport. Everything tastes different here.

Chapter 2

"I'm scared," I whispered to Paul, and grabbed his hand.

The scent of musky floral incense hung in the early morning air outside the airport terminal. Taxi drivers were screaming in words that seemed to have no beginning or end.

"Let's have a smoke," Paul said. A cigarette always helped to calm me down. We dropped our backpacks to the ground. "Look after the bags, sweetheart. I'll go get some fags." His lanky figure disappeared back inside the terminal and I felt panicky. I had no cell phone and was in charge of two bags too heavy to carry, much less run away with if I had to.

It had taken Paul only a couple of hours to pack for this trip, but for me it took days. We were embarking on a year-long-adventure around the world. It felt impossible to limit myself and choose only a few items when everything felt necessary. I wanted to be ready for every circumstance. Paul had a rule of thumb: "If you can't fit one small pillow on top of your pile, then you've packed too much." He knew best for this kind of thing. First, he was twenty-eight, older than me by six years. And second, he had backpacked with his mates before. Peru, Guatemala, Brazil—they had been everywhere. He was like Indiana Jones.

When Paul came back his forehead was glistening and his shirt had darkened under the armpits.

"I'm already sweating like a pig," he said. He opened the carton and handed me a pack before shoving the rest in his backpack. He wiped his large forehead with his shirtsleeve, lit my cigarette first and then his. Even though it was the same brand, it smelled and tasted sweeter than the ones we smoked in Europe. I took a few drags and wondered if there was some kind of spice in the cigarette or if the flavor came from outside.

The yelling around us intensified, as the taxi drivers gestured wildly. They were fighting over who would get the next ride. No one seemed in charge. I thought of the English and their queues. Although their rigidness sometimes frustrated me, I was already starting to miss that sense of order.

Paul took his camera out, put a roll in, and clicked it three times before taking snaps of the scene.

"It'll be fun, Coco," he said, as if guessing my thoughts. He ran his fingers through my hair and I relaxed. His touch was better than a cigarette. My hair was shorter than I had asked for at the salon—above my shoulders—but I was glad for the change. I needed something tangible to mark the end of my assisting year at school.

"Are you sure it's not too short?" I asked. I was worried I didn't look as feminine without my long blonde waves.

"It'll grow back fast."

Paul's answer wasn't very reassuring. We were on a trip that symbolized our commitment to each other and I needed to know that he'd be there for me, with me, next to me, all the way through.

He put his camera down. "You're always beautiful, no matter how short or long your hair is. Mum says you could be a model."

He smiled, turned his attention to the taxi drivers and took a few more photos.

I took in the new wave of tourists that walked out of the terminal and the mess of screaming drivers and honking horns. They looked as stunned as I felt.

"I told you it was going to be a culture-shock," Paul said.

I now understood what he meant.

If visiting other European countries had seemed foreign to me at times, Asia felt like an excursion to an alien land. But I was excited: for one year of my life, I was going to live free of any duties and responsibilities. I still had to take a teaching qualification exam at some point, but there would be no class to assist, test to take, or rent to pay this year. I was far away from my parents, my roommates, and my day-to-day routine. I had a year to decide where my future would lie—France or Britain. The present was freedom. Pure freedom.

Paul flicked his cigarette butt, picked up his bag, handed me mine and said, "Stay close to me." We walked through the crowd of screaming drivers and settled with one who offered us, in English, what sounded like the most reasonable rate to the hotel. Paul bargained an even cheaper taxi fare once we got in. I loved that side of him, so practical and adventurous. We were on a really tight budget, me in particular, but Paul's parents had paid for a night in a hotel and we had agreed to take a taxi for our first ride in Thailand.

On the back seat next to me, Paul grinned. "Did you notice that they drive on the *right* side of the road too?"

The traffic was worse than in Paris or anywhere else I had been, except maybe Rome. "Yes, they *too* are crazy," I answered. "You'll be fine here." We enjoyed teasing each other. I leaned over to kiss him, but he pulled away.

"Remember, sweetheart, no PDA in Thailand."

I sat back, disappointed. I didn't think we'd have to observe the rule even in a taxi. My French ways and his Englishness did not always complement each other. He gave my knee a squeeze and mocked a pout until I finally smiled back at him.

I was sitting on the patio at Paul's place one winter evening, a blanket over my lap with a glass of wine in one hand and a cigarette in the other when Paul said, "What would you say if I asked you to come traveling with me for a year?" My heart skipped. I didn't want to go back home to France; I wanted to stay with Paul even though we had only been dating for a few months. "That way, you won't have to leave when your job at school ends." Neither of us wanted to have a long distance relationship and the thought of being apart from Paul was heart wrenching. Leaving behind everything I knew sounded very scary but at the same time, exciting. "I'd say yes!" I yelled, so loudly that a stray cat near my feet jumped over the brick wall into the neighbors' garden.

If our love could survive a trip like this, Paul said, we could think of a future together. He filled our glasses with more wine and we went to bed dizzy and excited, with full displays of affection. After we made love I imagined us strolling through bazaars, holding hands, feeding each other noodles on the beach and climbing mountains, knowing that I was going to be safe with him because he had just promised to take care of me.

The day following Paul's proposal, we went to buy a map—not just a piddling map of Europe, but a map of the *whole* world—and laid it out on the thick white carpet of the living room, pushing the coffee table and armchair aside. We knelt down with pen and paper and made a list of the places we always dreamt of going. It felt like writing a Christmas list.

"I've always wanted to go to Vietnam."

"Well, just put it down. Where else, sweetheart?"

"Australia! Tibet! China! What about India? I really want to go to India."

"Might be hard for a first time backpacker like you," he answered.

A little disappointed, I kept going with my pen. "Maybe Alaska. Yes, Alaska!" I ignored Paul's smirk. "And Uruguay, and Paraguay, and Bolivia, and…"

Once we had let all of our thoughts float high enough, reality set in—we were not millionaires and we couldn't take ten years off. To help us narrow down the itinerary, Paul suggested we choose places where we could visit some of his friends. One of them, Simon, lived in Bangkok.

"Here we are." Paul pointed at a large white gate, the entrance to the Bangkok Hilton. We looped around the driveway, framed by bushes and red flowers and a spectacular tower adorned with a giant white staircase suddenly appeared.

"Oh la la! I've never stayed at a place like that. The only hotel we would stay at with my parents, when we were not camping, was the old Formule 1. It was cheap as chips! Less than a hundred francs a night."

"How come you're still counting in francs? I know the euro better than you do—that's not normal."

"It's still new. And until last year, they still showed both prices at the store, so I didn't have to make any effort."

The taxi pulled in front of the red-carpeted staircase where three doormen in red and gold uniforms stood. One of them opened the car door for me, while another went to the trunk to help with our bags. Were we still in the same country? After we checked in, a bellhop took us to our room. A thick red carpet covered the floor and carved wooden mirrors decorated the walls. Paul handed the man a few dollars and closed the door. I walked to the balcony and slid open the doors to admire the hotel grounds below. Two long rows of hibiscus led to a swimming pool, in front of which the premise of a wedding reception was being set up. A two-meter-long sign bearing the name of the couple, written in big colorful letters, hung above the stage. I could imagine young "Yok and Pop" murdering the dance floor in the evening to the Sophie Ellis-Bexter song that was already playing outside. I then pictured what my wedding with Paul would look like: a chocolate cake on a large table in a barn, dancing to Culture Club's Karma Chameleon, Mum shedding tears, Dad telling me how proud he was, Paul lifting the veil...

"If we were in England, everybody would already be drunk by now." Paul was leaning over the railing. "And in the pool." He laughed. Would his friends be drinking at 1 p.m.? Would he? "C'mon," he said, and closed the door, "let's get out and explore."

"No," I said, "you come on." I kissed him, releasing all the frustration I had felt earlier. "It's not public here." I could see his eyes wandering to his camera. Determined, I took him by the hand and pulled him close to me on the bed.

Chapter 3

The mosquito bites on my legs are itching and the lights of the Brooklyn Bridge shine too bright through the bare window. Still on Southeast Asian time, I've been awake for an hour. I stare at Andrew's bedroom—*our* bedroom, as he corrected me. It needs something: some curtains or a painting on the wall, perhaps. The apartment has been newly renovated with a stainless steel kitchen, a sound system in every room, rain shower and mini-sauna. It is much more spacious than the apartment I was renting in midtown with a girl I met on Craigslist. I'd like to paint a wall, but Andrew won't have any color here. He wants to keep it neutral in case he decides to sell it sooner than later. He has freed two extra shelves so I now dispose of more than half the closet space. I had sorted through my clothes and filled two huge bags for the Salvation Army; I didn't need the extra space but I appreciate his effort to try and make me feel at home.

I switch on the light, but I have no book and no bedside table. When we were little, my sister and I, read every night before going to bed. It helped me relax and sleep better. I did not sleep at all on the flight home from Thailand and now, two days later, I'm struggling with jet lag. Andrew is sound asleep. The muscle relaxant tablets he takes knock him out. I don't want to lie here and wait, listening to him sleep. I throw on some clothes and head out.

The neighborhood is just waking up. I linger on the cobblestone streets, walk towards the Financial District and get a coffee and a croissant from a street vendor. Wall Street is closed to traffic: they're either shooting a movie or another episode of Law and Order. I cross over to the pier on the east river side. I've never been there at dawn. On Sunday afternoon, I used to go for a run with Andrew. We would start from the Seaport, follow the southern tip of Manhattan and run up along the west side. I miss those moments of quiet connection between us.

An engine roars from the water and sends seagulls flying south. A ferry, en route to Brooklyn, pulls away from the pier. I take a seat on a bench in the middle of the esplanade and take it all in. I can almost feel the vibrations in the sky, orange like the soil in the Australian desert. The sky stretches, pulling shades of pink to its extremities. If I had my own place, these are the colors I would use to paint the living room, a reflection of my more adventurous self.

A man with a stereo blaring Asian music walks by. I can't help but smile, remembering bus trips with music videos of Thai ballads. He drops his stereo to the ground just a few feet away from me. Another man on my right laughs and dances. He wants to pull me into his groove, but I shake my head no. A few minutes later, I am surrounded. Babies in strollers howl, elderly people warm up their bones and about a dozen other people get ready for their Tai Chi practice with blasting Chinese disco music. Everyone takes their spot, the instructor rolls his shoulders, babies quiet down and the people start to fall into the same rhythm.

A strong energy circulates, taking different tones and shapes. I feel it dance its way inside of me. I remain very still. I want to laugh and smile for no reason. I am reminded of children on the banks of the Mekong, waving hello for minutes that seemed like years and seconds at the same time. Then something else makes its way to my heart: a torrent of sadness. I let it pass through me without understanding why.

A few moments later, like a receding tide, people leave the esplanade. I stay and feel joy again. A similar sadness would sometimes envelop me when I traveled with Paul through Southeast Asia and Australia. Despite the beauty of the landscape, it would eat me. When we visited the Killing Fields, I was overcome with an urgent need to leave. Paul said I was so sensitive—as if it were a disease.

The pocket of my jacket vibrates. My agent from Hamburg is calling.

"I'm sorry, love. Nivea released you. Don't worry, I'm sure we'll get them next time."

I should be used to being rejected by clients—it's a part of modeling—yet it still stings. I recently spent three weeks and more than a few euros in Germany to try and get more bookings and new clients. I go every year but this time it was a less fruitful investment. The economic downturn is scaring companies away from marketing. The jobs are fewer, the rates are lower and only the competition, fierce as ever, remains unchanged.

So Nivea chose someone else—it's nothing personal. I have been modeling for five years and I still don't understand all the rules. Or rather, I'm still not comfortable with them. I remember what Morgan, a friend I made when I started out, told me: "You can't be everybody. You can't be blonde and brunette, skinny and have boobs. Don't compare yourself to others. You can only be you." Sarah, the girl I met in Thailand, sounds very much like her.

I'm cold now. I'm hoping to snuggle in bed with Andrew, but he's already left for work when I get back. Sarah has sent me a text; she's having a blast in Alaska and hopes that we hang out when she gets back in town. I do a load of laundry so I can pack the same clothes for my next tropical job and put my sneakers on to go for a run. I'm craving a cigarette.

Chapter 4

After we made love, we stayed in bed and leafed through a copy of Lonely Planet: Thailand. We mapped our plans for the afternoon and then Paul brought up the concept of "saving face" in Thailand again.

"You'll have to get used to it, sweetheart." He lowered his gaze and put his hand on my thigh. "Coco, you know that I love you?" I nodded. My heart skipped a beat. "But I've got to be honest—I'm not so keen on being touched so much." He looked up and must have seen the pain on my face. "What I'm trying to say is that I need a little space, you know. It's normal. Like I'm sure you need space too."

"What's the point of being together then if I can never touch you?"

"Sweetheart, I didn't say never… just… not as much, that's all."

I tried to put on a good face. He got out of bed and sorted through the rolls of film in his camera bag.

Taking a year off after high school or college to go traveling was a pretty common thing in England, but not in France. The French did not see the necessity of having an adventure before being swallowed by the professional world. Apart from a few, like my dad, who knew that travels broadened the mind, most French believed that if you went traveling for so long, you weren't fit to work. I'd wanted to teach since the age of fifteen–I came from a family of teachers–I just wasn't sure where I wanted to teach. The decision depended greatly on how well Paul and I would get along on this trip. With his confession, it wasn't off to a great start.

I stared out the window at the hazy blue sky and the Bangkok skyline, and realized that if Paul wasn't on my side for this year away, I would be alone. Wings of anxiety knotted my stomach.

We went downstairs to the restaurant. A lunch buffet was included in our stay and although I wasn't very hungry now, I could not pass up a free meal. Afterwards, I put on my sunglasses, Paul took his camera and in the blazing sunshine, we left the hotel. Outside, a driver wanted to take us to the Emerald Buddha Temple, a magnificent place of worship, but our conversation in the bedroom had upset me too much to play the tourist. Paul bargained a good price for a simple tour around the city. We hoped in the three-wheeled tuk-tuk and drove off, carried by the strains of music from a transistor radio that sounded to me like old ballads.

In spite of our request, the driver took us to a temple in the heart of the city. The temple of the Sitting Buddha was small and humble compared to the popular temples. I liked that. Inside, we met a man who told us he was a bank manager. He told us about a special tax-free week in tones that suggested a holy revelation. When we left the temple and found our driver, he insisted on taking us to the mall for tourists but neither Paul, nor I wanted to go shopping.

"Just take a look," the driver said. "You don't have to buy. I get gasoline ticket and we go." Paul and I looked at each other suspiciously: something was fishy. "I take you to the shop and he gives me free gasoline ticket. You don't need to buy. Ok?" The guilt trip was on. We grudgingly agreed. We'd have to toughen up if we wanted to avoid more scams.

We headed into the chaotic traffic, weaving snakelike in and out of lanes, jostling for space. I held on tight to the rail above my head, while Paul, unperturbed, photographed the scene flashing by outside. I breathed in wafts of incense and rotten meat and diesel fumes. My hands were clammy, my seat was sticky and I loved it. I tilted and lowered my head half way out, marveling at the bustle unwinding before me. Bright and colorful flowers—offerings to Buddha—appeared everywhere. They lit up the streets inside large baskets, adorned the walls of temples, and balanced on rear view mirrors next to beaded necklaces and deity medallions.

We stopped at a tiny gas station in front of the mall. Someone came and handed our driver a ticket. He looked at us with a huge smile and started filling up the tank. The fumes were too strong to stay in the tuk-tuk, so Paul dragged me inside the first store in the mall. I thought we were just killing time in the jewelry section when Paul called me over to one of the display cabinets. He pointed at a shiny ring.

"But it's all a scam," I protested.

"I know, but who cares. I want you to have something beautiful."

"It's a lot of money."

He shrugged his shoulders. Did he feel bad about hurting my feelings earlier on? "Just try it on," he said.

I was reassured. He still loved me. I had known him for only a year and was aware that we had rushed it a bit, but Paul was the one. He was an artist with a real job: a talented photographer who also worked in a photographic equipment store and taught photography classes on weekends. He was wonderful to his niece and nephews and he wanted to be with me, explore with me, go to the far corners of the world with me. What more could I wish for?

The ring was a perfect fit.

Later that afternoon, after a leisurely stroll in Lumpini Park, we asked our driver to take us to the compound of Wat Arun, a Khmer-style tem ple with ornately carved spires and colorful porcelain. We ate Tom Yum soup by the river and waited for nightfall when the Loy Krathong festival would begin. To celebrate the full moon, families had gathered for lantern-lit picnics. Paul went to take pictures of school children performing traditional dances and playing cymbals and xylophones. It made me think of the many craft projects I had done with kids when I was a summer camp counselor in between my college years. It was one of the most challenging jobs I had ever done, being on call 24/7 for weeks at a time, but it was also the most rewarding—their hugs, their tears, my tears… There was no doubt that I would teach. I wanted to feel that sense of connection year round and take them from one place to another, watch them grow and open up to the world and to themselves.

The crowd grew on the lawn. People were praying, chatting, selling and buying flowers. All day, Thai people had assembled flower bouquets for this special event. Kneeling on the river bank, they closed their eyes and sung to their many gods what I guessed were prayers of gratitude. I envied their faith.

I lay down and took a close look at my ring, a sapphire solitaire with tiny, diamond-like stones. I held my hand up to the sky where it blended with the stars.

Paul and I had met at an art gallery where some of his portraits and landscapes were being exposed. I liked how he licked his lower lip and raised his hands when he discussed his photography to those who asked about his wide-angle technique or the places he had been to. I waited for him to come and talk to me, and we kissed later in front of the Trafalgar Square fountain. Magic was in the air from that night on.

I sat up. Paul was fixing a new roll in his camera, sticking his tongue out for concentration, like children do. I bought a small bunch of flowers with a candle. Paul found me in front of the stall and together we went to the river. In the dark of night, people had clustered along the Chao Phraya River to let the small vessels of flowers, candles and incense that floated on banana leaves shine up to the moon. The temple was illuminated by the people's gifts to the river—they were giving back to her what she had given them all year round: an abundance of blessings. I felt a deep joy witnessing the celebration and also a longing for a personal way to connect with something I could sense was larger than me.

Chapter 5

Our night of luxury at the Hilton was over. The adventure took a new turn when I heaved my backpack on my shoulders to hike from the bus station to the youth hotel. It was heavier than I could bear. The heat added itself to the load.

"You're alright?" Paul asked.

My legs wobbled and the muscles of my neck and shoulders burned with fatigue. Even my finger hurt, swollen and compressed underneath the ring. "All good," I said.

The hostel was in the middle of a large and rather quiet street, considering how noisy the city was. The common area was a cozy wide-open space that made me feel more comfortable than the shiny and ornate entrance of the Hilton. A small kitchen in the back gave way to a second-hand library on the right. I had rehearsed with Paul what to ask the innkeeper. She told us the night and weekly rates, what time breakfast was served until, and how to get laundry service. She showed us the rooms upstairs. It would have been cheaper to stay in the dormitories, but what would have been the point of traveling together if we had to be separated? Our double room was a very simple, Spartan setup: a bed, a toilet, a sink and a showerhead. There was no bathroom door, pillows, or bedclothes, just an old fitted sheet on a mattress, stained with yellow spots and pocked with holes.

"Is this ok, sweetheart?"

I was glad to have found a cheap place. "As long as we're together, I'm fine." I unpacked a few things: my toiletry bag, my blue dry towel and a clean shirt. I pulled one picture out of the fold inside the notebook Manu, my sister, had bought me and smiled at the image of the two of us, our foreheads touching—a photo booth souvenir from the year before. We did not look much alike and yet it was easy to tell we were sisters. Perhaps what Paul and I needed, before we could be as tender as we were to each other back home, was just a little time to adjust to our new environment.

A couple of hours later, we entered the jungle of Koh San Road. Thai music burst through speakers hung to electric poles, stapled with their local superstars' posters. They looked like covers of romance novels. This was where Simon, Paul's friend, told us to meet him. Koh San Road was a street mentioned in every tourist brochure. Travel agent's desks were lined up one after the other, like a bunch of fishermen waiting for backpackers to take the bait. The heat and hubbub from the street made my head spin. My manners, my dress code and even just my fair blonde head, taller than most, made me feel uncomfortable.

We passed tourist stands loaded with piles of pants and pashminas in every color. The street was packed with tourists and backpackers in light cotton pants and headbands that gave them a Hippie-Thai style—a mix of east and west. What did the Thais think of me? Another tourist? A stupid tourist who thinks she understands our culture or just cha-ching?

Paul, on the other hand, was much more at ease and familiar with this kind of traveling. It created a distance between us that I couldn't explain to him, but that made me feel a little foreign to him too.

An hour of madness passed before Simon, accompanied by Lana, the girl he lived with, came to the rescue. At a street café, he ordered beer for all of us. The waitress came back with four glasses half-filled with ice. I poured in my beer and cooled off instantly.

"We're talking of opening a bar together," Simon said. "Maybe in Koh Samui."

"You're never coming back to London, mate?" Paul asked.

"No intention of ever being a banker again."

"But how are you going to live?" I asked.

"Life in Thailand is easy," Simon explained. "You don't need much to be happy here. Everything is cheap. I worked out that, with my savings, if I sold a minimum of two beers a day in my bar, I could live off that till I'm seventy."

"And what happens after, if you live longer?" I asked.

Lana giggled. "We'll have children to take care of us."

I chuckled. It wasn't how we were told to think in the west.

"Are you guys going to Vietnam?"

"I was just talking about that with Coline," Paul said. "But we need to leave our passports at the embassy for a week if we do."

"Why don't you head to Koh Chang while you wait for your visa? That's what I did when I first came here."

"Yes, very nice," Lana said. "Take a bus, it's cheap."

I was hungry and peeked at the menu. It was all in Thai.

"We'll let you order for us," Paul said.

"You like spicy or not too spicy?" Lana asked me.

"Not too spicy," I was quick to answer.

She giggled. She giggled all the time, about anything. It was a little unnerving.

The waitress came with five dishes for us to share. I tried the green curry and added many spoons of rice to tame the spice. There was fried rice with pork, roasted duck and some salad.

"No chopsticks?" I asked Lana, while scanning the other tables.

"It's for tourists," she said and let out another giggle. "We use forks and spoons. Like you." She held out a chicken satay dish for me. "You want to come to my house tomorrow night for dinner? Real Thai." She laughed again and I knew I should be worried. "My mum wants to invite you."

We went back to Koh San Road. I relied on Paul and Simon's bargaining skills to get us reasonable bus tickets to Koh Chang, while Lana took me shopping. A simple cloth attached to a pole worked as a changing room. She tried on a skirt I found much too short and disappeared back into the changing room. Just at that moment, someone caught my eye. The facial features had the perfection of a Barbie doll, the eyebrows were groomed and penciled, the eyes dark and smoky and yet I couldn't tell if she was a he or vice versa. Lana emerged from the changing room and saw me staring. I couldn't take my eyes off of him or her.

"Lady-boy," Lana said, by way of explanation.

He brushed his hair off his shoulders and shopped the rack, swaying his tiny hips with the elegance of a lady. It seemed forced yet graceful. Another lady-boy came out of a different changing room and stared at himself in the mirror, his mouth slightly open, as if ready to be kissed or flirting with his own reflection. He was beautiful. The glamorous pair suddenly burst out laughing. Boys being boys, I thought.

As the night wore on, I couldn't handle the Thai music that seemed to be everywhere. It was a relief to go back to the hostel and take a shower. I slipped off my ring and placed it carefully in the zip pocket of my toiletry bag. Simon had taken me aside earlier on. "I wouldn't wear it in the city," he said. "It'll attract the wrong crowd." I told Paul I would wear it again as soon as we left Bangkok.

I stepped into the shower and let the water run over my feet. "Bébé," I called, "come see." Paul obliged. "Look, it's all black." I said. "Imagine what gets in our lungs."

He stared at me from head to toe. "You dirty girl."

"Hey!"

He took his clothes off and stepped in the shower with me.

Paul fell asleep quickly after we made love. He always did. Outside, the traffic sounds kept me awake. Doors swung shut in the hostel as other residents came back, loud and laughing. I scribbled a few notes in my journal, the names of the places we had been to, and I stuck in the beer label I had detached earlier from a drink at a bar. I felt overwhelmed with the strangeness of everything I had seen, heard and tasted.

Chapter 6

In a bathroom mirror at Miami airport, I stare at my reflection and then pull out a wet wipe to remove the black kohl pencil around my eyes. Another wipe and the foundation comes off. This is my ritual: peeling off the modeling mask and stepping back into my normal person skin. I'll only keep the make up on if I'm going out later with Andrew. My face now clean, I layer moisturizer over a serum and top it all off with eye cream as expensive as my phone bill. Andrew gives me free products from the company he works for, but they contain too many chemicals—I buy my own, from an all-organic company.

I place all my small containers of skincare products—just the right size for airport security—back in a plastic bag and brush my hair. The heavy hairspray and beach wind have tangled it so much that it's best to tie it in a bun. If there were showers at the airport, I'd gladly pay for the service. I take another wet wipe and freshen my armpits, remove my contact lenses, and put my glasses on before leaving the restroom.

The departure screen shows a short delay for my flight. Two large women take a seat across from me and nibble on a giant warm pretzel and BBQ chicken wings. I'm craving coffee and a cigarette. A/C blows cold air on my neck. I unfurl my scarf, a large swathe of earthy brown cotton fabric embroidered with small white irregular patterns that I bought in Thailand. I sprayed Andrew's cologne on one corner of it before leaving to Miami. It still smells of him, woody and musky. As if on cue, he calls.

"We got Japan!"

I congratulate him on this long awaited deal. He's been working on the account since the beginning of the year. "I finished work early, my flight gets in around six," I say. "We can leave for Hudson this evening and celebrate your success together."

"The company is throwing a little party tonight. I don't want to be driving on a Saturday—there'll be too much traffic. We'll go another weekend, yeah?"

"Of course. Yes. That's great. I'm very excited for you."

After he hangs up I cancel the hotel. I'm disappointed, but Christmas is less than two months away. It'll go by fast.

The line for a cab at La Guardia is short, thank goodness. It's cold out, especially after being in the Miami sunshine for a few days.

"Where to?" the man at the head of the taxi lane asks.

"Downtown. Corner of Beekman and Front Street."

Within minutes, I'm in a taxi, headed to Andrew's—our place. We take the Williamsburg Bridge, loop down and around the Lower East Side and head to the Seaport. As usual, there is construction work on every other street. The city will be great when it's finished, people joke, knowing it never will be.

The doorman welcomes me back. He always asks where I've been. There's a huge box beside the apartment door. My name is on the label and there's a photo of the fold-up bike I've been wanting. And in that moment my disappointment about the cancelled weekend getaway disappears. I drag the box inside with my luggage and tear it apart with a knife. I lay all the pieces on the hallway rug and start assembling my very own Batmobile.

Chapter 7

Lana and her mum lived in a part of Bangkok we probably wouldn't have visited on our own. Tucked away on a dark narrow street, Thai music faint on a faraway speaker, I reached for Paul's hand.

"This looks like it," he said uncertainly as Lana greeted us at the door with a bowing salute. We imitated our host and repeated the exchange with her mum and then with Simon. I offered Lana a little box of caramels from Normandy—my mum had sneaked them in my backpack when Manu and my parents came to say goodbye to us at Heathrow. Chocolates would have melted. Lana invited us to sit down on the floor around a low table. I tried to make myself comfortable propped against a triangle cushion, but nothing felt natural; there was an order to things that I couldn't grasp. Simon handed me a glass of beer with ice cubes.

"We did not cook everything," Lana explained. "It's cheaper to buy in street. They make big servings."

She placed three large dishes in the middle of the table. Simon did not wait for the ladies to join and started eating straight from the dishes with a fork. Paul and I hesitated. Lana said her mum would not join us for dinner and told us to help ourselves. I spooned some breadfruit and chicken curry in a small plate.

"Ouuuh la la!"

The rich creamy coconut sauce, seductive at first, hid some powerful heat. My French made them laugh. Simon poured more beer into my glass and assured me that I'd get used to it. Paul heaped more curry on his plate looking like a pig in muck.

My mouth was on fire but I tried the other dishes, full of ginger, lemongrass, coriander, fish sauce, chili, turmeric. I found it hard to concentrate on the conversation because my eyes kept watering and I grew flushed.

I turned to Paul. "Don't you find this super spicy?"

"It's a little hot," he said.

That was it? Just a little hot? He saw the tears rolling down my cheeks, wiped them with his napkin and smiled tenderly. I put my fork down to take a breather. I'd be able to focus on what was being said, at least for a moment, as the talk had turned to the lady-boys.

This afternoon again, we had encountered a group of young men dressed like women, with beautifully made up faces. The lightness of their stride, the slight swaying movement of their slender hips, the way they carried themselves, shoulders back and head straight, and the awareness they had of their effect on others, amazed me. Compared to my own feelings of self-consciousness, they seemed to know more about being a woman than I did.

"They're an integral part of society," Simon said. "I went to the bank the other day and the teller was a lady-boy. Some of them are strippers or prostitutes but many have regular jobs. They're accepted here, it's not like trannies back home. They even have beauty contests."

"So, do you say *he* or *she?*" I asked, taking a bite from a slice of pineapple.

"They feel like women, so you should say *she*," Simon answered. "Actually they want to be assimilated as a third sex—men, women, and lady-boys. Are you ok, Coline?"

"Yes," I said, tears in my eyes yet again. What were spices doing on a pineapple? I coughed and cried, "I'm fine. Please—continue." I shot-gunned another beer. Paul placed a hand over my back in a soothing gesture.

When we wished them goodnight outside Lana said, "If you turn right, female strippers. If you go left, lady-boys."

"Is there another way?" I asked, smiling.

"You can go straight," Simon answered with a wink.

Koh-Chang was supposedly the most untouched tropical forest in Southeast Asia. The bus ride to the ferry, which should have only been a five-hour-journey southeast from Bangkok, was a *tad* longer, as Paul would say, and bumpier than promised. It was double the time. I hoped it would all be worth it once we arrived. I had been dreaming of a walk on the beach with Paul, hand in hand, swimming together and kissing under water. We had never had a beach vacation together, except for a short trip to Brighton and I looked forward to spending time alone with him. Away from the big city, he would relax with me like he used to, I hoped. As soon as we arrived at our lodge, I would put my ring back on.

We missed the first boat and arrived at the dock in Trat in time for the late afternoon ferry. Onboard, I met a young girl who told me about the rubber business her mum owned.

"I have to get up at one in the morning to collect the tree sap," she said. "But that's when the rubber is better."

She gestured to show me the diagonal slash she made in the tree. "Then you wait for the white rubber to come out in a bucket."

I tried imagining my mum working in the rubber business instead of teaching Latin, and asking Manu and me to help her in the middle of the night. When she was a little girl, Mum had to milk the cows in the morning and then ride her bike to school for long, hilly kilometers. Was my childhood too easy? School was always within walking distance and all I had to do in the afternoon was my homework. If I had endured more, perhaps I would have been stronger. I hated to admit it, but so far I had been finding our backpacking trip hard.

"What about your dad," I asked. "What does he do?"

"He's a fisherman. He has a boat just like those ones," she said, pointing to a small, random fleet on the gulf.

My dad would have lost his mind if he had been put on a boat to fish. He thrived on being constantly challenged with new projects at work. Budgeting, making plans and previsions seemed like what he was born to do.

The sea harbored hundreds of fishermen boats, all brightly lit to attract fish at night. The sun plunged into Hat Kai Bay, the sea and sky merging into one dark sheet on fire—the father and mother of all things uniting, making us the guardians of their secret. It was dark when we reached the secluded hut on the beach that Paul had arranged for the week and we stumbled through the undergrowth with just a flashlight. This part of the beach was private, with no existing path from the main road to the bungalows. I looked up—stars were falling from the sky. France and England were very far away.

I woke up in the morning covered in mosquito bites. Paul barely had any. He said it was my fault for being so sweet. I opened the door of the bungalow and stared at the patch of paradise we had landed in. I walked on the white sand beach and eased myself into the pristine water like a woman slipping into a silk gown. The aches from my backpack, the thin mattress, the hard, uneven floor, all disappeared in the warm salty water. Heaven seemed closer on a beach.

After lunch, I finally sat down to organize a daily budget. Dad would have been proud. I created columns for food and drinks, accommodation and transportation. The budget was tight and did not include a category for a barber, so when Paul passed his hand through his thick brown hair and said he needed a haircut, I said, *"Pas d'problème. I have nail scissors!"* I set up a little salon on the terrace. Paul took his shirt off and faced the sea. We were like two castaways. "How little one needs to be happy," I said. Paul turned around and looked at me with love in his eyes.

In the afternoon, we went on an elephant tour through the jungle. I rode an elephant named Moon who kept flapping her ears against my feet. She would rather have eaten pomelos, sweet giant grapefruits, than played that tourist circus. She was treated like a slave, poked and scratched until she bled behind her tired ears, and I felt conflicted about the ride. Surely we were also the perpetrators of that injustice. Back in the small hut where she was chained up I fed her with bananas, the only sweet thing I could do to ask for forgiveness.

The days on the island went by fast. The last evening began as the fantasy I had had before leaving London, eating Pad Thai on the beach, candles and ornaments adorning the trees around us. Christmas wasn't far off, but the trees here were decorated year round, our waitress told us. After dinner, we left the restaurant and wandered into the town. It was small but lively: bars and restaurants all had large screens playing movies, and the proximity of these places and the open plan made for a cacophony of competing sounds and pictures. Paul wanted to watch the last Tarantino movie. He agreed that I could wake him up later if I had a nightmare, which was a likely outcome. We walked back to one of the first bars on this noisy strip, sat down, ordered beer and turned our chairs to face the TV screen. Everyone laughed when a ninja sliced people's feet off. I turned my face away, horrified.

"You're taking it too seriously," Paul said. He ordered another beer. I wasn't even half way done with mine. It was too violent to be funny. We stayed till the end and I insisted on taking a long walk on the beach before heading back to our hut. I held his hand tight. Paul was tired but I was nervous, unable to digest the scary images. Why were we such a violent race?

Lying in bed, I couldn't breathe. I couldn't move.

"What are you afraid of?" Paul asked.

"Everything. Someone could come in—the door doesn't lock—a thief, a rapist, an assassin, who knows?"

"Where do you—I don't understand you sometimes. We just had such a nice evening and now you're all freaked out."

"What was nice about that movie? It's not my fault—you know I can't handle too much violence."

"You're so sensitive."

"I know."

His eyes softened. "I'm sorry, sweetheart. What would make you feel better?" His voice was deep and reassuring.

"Would you read aloud from your book for me, please?"

Paul smiled and obliged. I didn't care about what he was reading. I curled up in his arms, my head on his chest, listening to his heartbeat and slowly I began to relax.

A mini-bus rocked us back to civilization after five days in paradise. The passengers were a mixed bag: A Thai woman prayed incessantly–I imagined that she was praying for the bus not to flip, which, considering the suspension, was highly plausible. There was also a young French woman, a semi-professional backpacker on a journey through Asia. She would spend the first six months of the year in France saving up money so she was able to travel for the next six months. Her face was a little weathered and her clothing was very simple. A man who worked for an oil company, some newly-weds on their honeymoon and an old European man with a young Thai girl made up the rest of the passengers. On a small bench at the back of the bus, holding on tight to the handle bar above my head and coughing from the dust, I wondered what people thought of Paul and me when they met us. Would they have described us just an English guy and a French girl? What else could they see?

The French woman was only a few years older than me. Did she enjoy traveling by herself? Why was she doing it alone? Did she want to be alone or had she never found anyone she would happily live with? As much as I didn't understand her, I envied her strength of character.

"Once, I was in the jungle," she spoke in English. Her accent was very thick, but her voice so calm–no one laughed or commented on how cute she sounded. "I had planted my tent in a rice field. In the middle of the night, I heard footsteps. I got dressed, very fast and I stayed there, ready to fight. Then I heard a voice."

I held my breath.

"It was the farmer. He was worried for me. He wanted to make sure I was ok."

Back in Bangkok, Paul and I settled back in the same youth hostel we had left a week before. The Vietnamese embassy had stamped our passports with the necessary tourist visas. We did not need to worry about Laos and Cambodia for now and were free to keep traveling in Southeast Asia. I changed into a new pair of Thai pants I had bought on the island and fixed a bandeau in my hair, thick and wavy with the constant humidity in the air. Paul went to check his emails and I went to the phone booth outside and called home.

"You received a letter from the University Institute," Mum said.

"How much time do I have to answer?"

"You have until June. That's nine months. But why don't you answer now?"

"I just want to keep my options open."

"I suppose England is not far… You could teach there."

I suppressed the urge to tell her I'd do what I wanted to do. "Yes."

"How are you and Paul getting along?"

"We're fine. How's Dad?"

"Good. Busy with work, as usual. Meetings after meetings, it's the season. I can't do anything about it. He doesn't listen when I tell him he needs to take things easier."

The communication was cut short¬—my credit had gone by faster than I thought. The evening light made everything look pretty outside. I leant against a wall in the street, pulled my notebook out and wrote about the colorful baskets of fruits in the market, the people sleeping in the streets, the dust and dirt and the people sweeping in front of their shops, the incessant honking and loud language. I started writing about my feelings, but stopped. If I were to build some resilience like I wanted, I should not give my doubts and anxieties so much attention. Writing or talking about them would only create more whining. I wanted Paul to think of me as someone he could rely on.

I went back to our room at the hostel to pick up the travel guide but did not find it there. I wanted to map out our next trip up north. I found Paul in the library, studying the guide, and put my arms around him.

"Coline!"

"What? I just…"

"Give me space, will you?"

I swallowed hard. My feelings welled up in my throat.

An American couple came into the library; I recognized the nasal accent. The woman sat at my table by the window. She had the same travel guide as us. I asked her how long they had been on the road. Maybe they could suggest an itinerary to follow.

"Six months now, right, Mark?" she said to her partner.

Mark was looking at picture books on the shelves. He nodded, smiled and sat down so that the four of us were now forming a circle in the room. It was unusual for Americans to be traveling for such a long period of time, but Mark and Kate were not the usual backpackers. Within the span of a few months, Kate had lost both her parents and Mark had been laid off after working for fifteen years for the same company. It was time for them to finally take this long vacation they had been putting off for years. Mark spoke of their adventures through Russia and China and Paul's face lit up. Soon he and Mark went to get beers, while I stayed and chatted with Kate. She pointed at the route they had been following and recommended we take the train up to Chang Mai. She highlighted the villages along the way that she had liked and paused. "I don't know why we waited so long to take this trip," she said. "You think that your job and a hundred other things are so important when really, they're not." I felt her pain but didn't know how to respond. "It's about the connections you make in life." The guys came back. I tried to make eye contact with Paul but he avoided me.

"Kate came down with a really bad fever one day," Mark said. "We were hiking in China. She was freezing. We came upon some villagers, we were so lucky, right, honey?" Mark and Kate exchanged a wink. "They took us back to their huts and cared for her like we were part of their community. These people were poor, extremely poor, but they asked for nothing in return. We offered them money, but they wouldn't take it."

Another hour and another round of beer and cigarettes went by until Mark and Kate had to leave to go to a show they had gotten tickets for in advance. Paul and I went to bed.

When Paul would not talk to me, the world might as well collapse. It would have hurt all the same. There was nothing I could do to change Paul's attitude and lighten up the atmosphere between us. I felt stuck. If I probed, he retreated further, which pushed me into isolation. I didn't know if that was a boy/girl thing or if it was just us. All I knew was how much it hurt and that was worse than being scared.

He finished the last pages of his book and turned off the light.

"I feel a little lonely, you know," I said. I couldn't help it. It was too heavy to bear.

"What do you mean? I'm right here."

"Not alone. Lonely. It's different, no?"

"Come here," he said. I moved a little closer to him and waited. "I'm sorry. I lost a whole roll of photographs this afternoon. I don't know what happened." I was sorry for him. "I'll buy a digital camera tomorrow. There are some that aren't too pricey."

I wasn't sure he was telling me what was really bothering him, but I felt better now that he was talking to me again. I cradled my head in his neck and eventually fell asleep.

Chapter 8

Andrew walks in with fire in his eyes an hour later. Beauty Apparel just signed a five-million-dollar-deal with Japan, which makes Andrew their top sales representative. He stops in the hallway to look at my bike. "An admirer?"

I pop open the bottle of Veuve Cliquot I just bought. "A lover, actually."

He grabs my ass before I can fill the glasses and I almost spill champagne on the floor. I put the bottle down and he digs his fingers into my skin through the fabric of my dress, satin and light. His breath is warm on my neck. He nibbles on my ear lobes and whispers how much he loves me. He knows how to disarm me with his charm. We kiss, French way, my way, deep and languorous. He lifts me up onto the counter top and slips a hand underneath my dress between my legs. His confidence–repulsive at times–is now so seductive. He unfastens his belt and unzips his trousers. I feel each of his muscles contract under the pressure of my thighs, until his body relaxes, a little too soon for me.

A waiter with a full tray deftly moves through the gathering on the terrace. "Champagne, Miss?" I take a flute just as Andrew sees Mike, his boss, at the bar.

"Wait!" I say, catching his fugitive hand. "Don't leave me, we just arrived."

"You know everyone here." He throws me a small kiss in the air, freeing his hand from mine.

"I don't *know* them," I whisper. "I only–"

He leaves and Mike's wife comes to greet me.

"Coco, honey!" Lauren says. "I haven't seen you since Josh's Bar Mitzvah this summer." She gives me a sort of kiss and a sort of hug. She smells of Chanel No.5. "Isn't this beautiful?" The skyline is impressive: the Chrysler building shines in front of us with electric lights as a substitute for the stars we can't see in the charcoal sky. "Come, I want to introduce you to Martha and Joan." She leans in and whispers, "their husbands are on the committee board."

I follow, out of duty to Andrew, and put on my best agreeable front.

"These are gluten free," Martha says, taking a toast from the tray.

"You probably have to watch what you eat, don't you, sweetie?" Lauren says in front of her assembly of friends.

"I eat anything," I quickly answer. "I have a big appetite." The women stare me down and I hold the stare, a skill I learned at castings. Lauren has a very slender figure, but the other two women are rather round. I smile to play my part. "But I exercise a lot, of course, to compensate." They all chuckle with relief.

The air is breezy, the band plays a mellow tune.

"Things are getting pretty serious between you and Andrew, right?" I nod politely. "He works so hard and everyone loves him so much at the office. Women are crazy about him, you know." Lauren is not just Mike's wife, she's also the head of P.R. for Beauty Apparel. "How long have the two of you been dating? Two years?"

"Two and a half, almost."

"Oh, how sweet! Remember, ladies, when we used to count the halves? It's so sweet."

"Have you two talked about marriage yet?" Martha asks.

"We've talked about it, but... there's no rush."

"How old are you?" Joan asks.

Money does not buy class. "Twenty-seven," I answer. I even throw in a smile. The music suddenly loud covers their blank response. I grab another glass from the same waiter.

"Andrew is going to love Japan," Lauren says.

I stare at her. "What do you mean?"

"He's going to be there for the store opening, just before Christmas."

I didn't know that was part of the deal. That means he's not going to fly with me to France. "That's fantastic," I say, "congratulations." I'm going to kill him. I excuse myself from the group. I down my glass and pluck another one from a passing waiter. I don't want to feel my anger and disappointment. This is what my life is going to be like: bullshit conversations, fast fuck, broken deals and the guilt of not being a girlfriend-wife supportive enough of her boyfriend-husband. One more sip of empty bubbles for me.

I lean over the terrace railing. The cool air numbs me for an instant. As if to remind me that New York is still an American city, the Empire State Building sports red, white and blue lights. When I walk to Battery Park to look at the Statue of Liberty, I feel there's a bit of France in New York, and I feel at home. It was there, by the Hudson River, that I met Andrew. He was training for the marathon. He stopped beside me and pretended to stretch his calves and hamstrings while he chatted me up. He oozed strength and confidence and I was quick, too quick perhaps, to accept his invitation for a drink later in the evening.

"Did it hurt, when you fell from heaven?" Andrew murmurs in my ear. His smell of whiskey, Prada and fresh sweat is too strong tonight.

"Lauren said you were going to Japan for Christmas. What the fuck is that about?" I did not mean to sound so aggressive.

"How much have you been drinking tonight, Leen?"

"What does it matter? You said–"

"I know what I said. I'm sorry I won't be able to go to France with your family, but please, let's talk about this at home, ok?"

"Don't talk to me like that!" He stares at me, embarrassed. "I'm going home." Disoriented, I make my way through the crowd to the elevator.

"What are you doing?" he says, catching me by the elbow.

"Going home," I say. I shake his hand off.

"Why?"

"I don't want to stay here and watch you fake it with all these people."

"What are you talking about? I'm not faking anything. And these people are also my friends."

"That's news! I thought you were working on getting a bonus and a promotion." I press the elevator button and my purse falls off my hand. "I hate all of this."

"What do you hate, Coline?" He picks up my purse. "People having a good time and celebrating, huh?"

I look away. I don't even know why I'm saying this. The elevator arrives. Andrew grabs my free wrist. I look at him with barely contained rage and he lets go.

"So you're leaving? Just like that?"

"Yes. I drank too much anyway. Isn't that what you said?"

"And what am I going to tell people? That my girlfriend is drunk, so she had to leave? Is that what you want me to tell them?"

"I don't care." I step into the elevator and he holds the door.

"What more do you want? This is it."

The doors close between us.

In the elevator, I push down my tears. I feel so ashamed of myself I could almost leave the city and never come back. I tell the doorman outside that I don't need a cab. I walk. I feel stuck, trapped in a golden prison. I walk into a deli and buy a pack of cigarettes. The radio is on: something about the IMF warning of a global meltdown. Suddenly it hits me, how ridiculous I am being when thousands of people are being laid off every day here.

A man hunched on the step of the building next door asks me for a cigarette. I keep a few and give him the pack. I stare blindly at the street and the cars passing by. The smoke tastes bitter. This is hard to quit.

Why was I so mean to Andrew tonight? He is always very supportive with my job. Am I being unfair? My head is spinning and the alcohol isn't helping. I feel so confused, like a stranger in my own life.

Chapter 9

Through the window in the train heading north from Bangkok, I contemplated the paddy fields on my right. The faces of the people we passed loomed long and sad. Men bent over the rice crops. Their backs took the shapes of the scythes they held up high and threw down in half moon motions as they slashed the tall grass. Women walked wearily on the side of the road. Children roamed around the rails. Why weren't they in school, learning and playing? It was 10 a.m. on a Tuesday–time for recess back in France. I thought of some of the students I had helped take their A-levels the year before: Nate's goofy, but always insightful answers during our one-on-one sessions, Sabrina's impeccable French that led to conversations way beyond the topic, and Geoffrey humoring me when I didn't know a word. I wanted to teach English, not French and I couldn't do that if I lived in England. I had to decide which teaching exam to take and this decision would affect my whole life, especially my relationships. Suddenly, I was not even sure that I still wanted to teach: I had never tried doing anything else.

A young monk in a yellow robe got on the train and took a seat across the aisle.

I never told anyone that I used to "pray" in bed. I would press my hands really tight together and beg for my wish to be granted. I sometimes believed that I was passing my exams thanks to those prayers. I needed to believe that things were going to be ok. That someone was watching out for me. It wasn't rational; it was quite childish even. Kant reassured me for a moment in high school—it was ok to believe, as long as we accepted that our beliefs were just beliefs. I thought then that God, religion, were just tricks of the mind so we could feel safe and be happy. But all the wars seemed to stem from religion, or rather intolerance towards different beliefs. By the time I went to college, I didn't want to believe in anything anymore. But I wished something could make sense to help me cope with the world—something that would make it less scary and lonely. I turned away to stare out my window, where people were working the fields. Space stretched mindlessly in front of me, the different landscapes sinking inside of me. We approached the old capital city of Ayuthaya, more modest in decorum than Bangkok. The city had been exhilarating, but too polluted and aggressive for me—I wanted to see the other Thailand.

We settled in the first guesthouse we saw in town. It was dirty—there only was one shower and two holes in the ground to share with the other guests—but it was cheap.

"It's fine for a night," I told Paul when he asked if I was going to be ok here. The window in our bedroom opened on to a brick wall, the concrete floor was bare and the walls were filthy. "It's part of the adventure, right?" I sat on the edge of the spring-less bed to look at the map. The old part of town was a sprawling complex of ruins large enough to bike around. The modern part of the city did not seem to be worth visiting, according to the guidebook. I suggested that we rent bikes in the afternoon. When I looked up at Paul, he was sweating profusely.

"Bloody Hell, I'm roasting." He wiped his face with the bottom of his shirt. We went outside to get iced coffees and found shade underneath a large mango tree on the terrace of a café adjoining our guesthouse. I pulled out my travel journal and Paul lit a cigarette. It was too hot to smoke for me. A warm breeze ruffled the leaves. We drank fast. Paul's face relaxed and we ordered a second round. At another table, a girl was chatting with an older man. She was traveling by herself and the man was advising her on the best route to follow. How did she manage? How did she deal with the nights spent alone? I felt I could almost travel by myself during the day, but nights scared me.

"Paul?"

Paul's eyes widened and sparkled. A young woman was striding toward our table, or more specifically, Paul, while her friend trailed behind her.

"Christy?" he stuttered and rose to his feet.

My straw was still in between my lips when they hugged. One of them said, "Oh my God!" and the other echoed it. An everlasting second passed before Paul introduced me. They had studied together in an art class years ago.

"What are the odds?" Paul said, awestruck.

Yes, really, what were the odds? It all sounded very rehearsed to me.

Christy wasn't alone. "We rented bikes for the day," her friend, Mia said.

"We were going to rent bikes too, weren't we, Col?" *Col?* Was that a new nickname or had he forgotten my name?

Paul sounded more excited about it now than he did when I suggested it.

"We can wait for you if you want," Christy said, without even giving a look in my direction. Mia didn't seem that enchanted about the group biking idea either.

Paul tried to get a sign from me. I kept my expression as passive as I could. "Let's meet later for dinner, *shall we?*" he said. I tried really hard to smile. Shall we? Really? In Thai culture, it's important not to lose face or argue in public. For me, it was important not to lose face in front of Paul and any other girl. Christy and Mia left on their bike and Paul and I sat back down.

I asked the question burning on my lips. "Did you two date in college?"

"What? Jesus Christ!" He lit a cigarette and stared out at the street.

"I'd rather know the truth. I can feel there was something between you—just tell me!"

"Oh, c'mon! Don't be ridiculous." He picked up his wallet from the table and shoved it in the pocket of his shorts. The disdain for me on his face saddened me no end. I packed my notebook and stood facing him, still waiting for his answer. "Why do you always have to create drama?" he said.

"This is so obvious! If you guys didn't have anything, why can't you just reassure me?"

He walked away, puffing furiously on his cigarette.

The air felt cooler as we rode our bikes later in the afternoon. We circled through the Old City, a wide-open space with dozens of temples and statues, many of which had been destroyed by the Burmese invasion in the 18th century. The breeze I felt in the alleys eased off the tension between us.

We started talking again. He liked the gold and cone shaped top of Phra Chedi Suriyothai and I preferred the simpler façade of the stupas and chedis that were composed of layers of burnt brick. Paul disappeared inside one of the temples while I tried to sketch a Buddha statue with a bright yellow piece of fabric tied around its waist. I did a terrible job of it. Were the fabric and flowers remnants of a ceremony or daily offering rituals for the inhabitants?

Click.

Paul took a picture of me. He looked in his screen, smiled and changed a few features on the body of his new toy before directing his attention to the headless statue next to me.

The positions of the Buddha statues were relaxed: sitting cross-legged, palms up, or reclining. No nails, no cross, no suffering. The freedom we were given to walk through that sacred place made me feel more connected to this culture than to Catholicism, the predominant and often intimidating religion in France. I could take the steps, touch the foundations, and even sit on the edges of the Buddhist temples. It was an invitation to a new experience.

We made our way to the Royal Palace, a grand building covered in its entirety in gold leaves. Paul chose to stay outside in the shade of a large mango tree. I went in. Against the back wall, a large bronze seated Buddha commanded the interior. Devotees whispered prayers. I was in some strange beautiful wonderland, scented with musk and flowers I had yet to identify. I watched in wonder, wishing I too could pray. I didn't know any prayers and didn't want to be disrespectful. On the front steps of the edifice a woman applied a gold leaf onto a small Buddha. Another one placed a lotus flower in a vase and a man lit an incense stick. I had never liked incense until that moment. Certain smells had to be experienced in the right places perhaps.

I searched for Paul–he wasn't under the tree anymore. I found him in a nearby square, listening to a kid play the violin. He handed me his water bottle. It was so hot that afternoon I thought I'd never stop sweating.

We met up with Christy and Mia at 7 p.m. We were walking down an especially dirty street when Mia pointed at a cooking station billowing smoke and said, "Let's have dinner here."

"Great," Paul said.

The ground was covered with rubbish. Sick-looking cats and dogs wandered among the stalls. "Is it safe to eat here?" I asked, trying to dissuade Paul.

"We eat like this every night," Christy replied.

I wanted to slap her.

"It's cheap, it's good and we're with the locals," Mia chimed in.

I wanted to slap her too.

Paul took in the whole market with one sweeping gesture and repeated how great this was. He had been taking pictures all day with me by his side but tonight with Christy and Mia he took none. Was I not as fun to be with as them? Paul had a weak stomach: I thought he might later regret having dinner here. For a minute, I almost hoped he got sick, but then quickly felt ashamed for even thinking such a thing.

I sat down on a small red plastic chair and tried to shake off the feeling I had of being the fourth wheel of some strange wagon. Music that played in the streets of Bangkok played here too, an almost familiar sound that now felt oddly comforting. Christy swooned over the pictures Paul had captured amongst the ruins earlier that day and she played for him a recording she had made from the streets in the new part of the city. Even though our travel guide had said that area was not interesting to visit, it was decided that we would go there tomorrow. The second beer I had did not help me relax any more than the first one did; I felt angry instead. I was also hungry, but I did not trust the chicken they had ordered.

Back at the guesthouse I tossed in my single bed, obsessing over the chemistry between Paul and Christy, wondering if the meeting hadn't actually been arranged. The mattress was hard and I couldn't get comfortable.

"Something happened between you," I said. I waited for a reaction from Paul lying in a separate bed. "Just tell me the truth."

"Nothing happened!" He inhaled deeply, put his book down, but kept it open in his hand and faced me. "She's just a very nice girl and we got along well. That's all there is to it." He went back to reading. I wished he hugged me, kissed me or told me something else, like how much he loved me, for instance.

I couldn't keep it in. I tried more softly. "I can sense there's something more. It's like an instinct. It's ok if that's the case, but it kills me to have the impression that you're lying to me." He threw his book on the bed. "Bloody hell, but you are absolutely mad!" His eyes had turned black. My jaw tightened. "Just quit it, will you?" He switched off his light and turned away from me. The silence was crushing. "I hate you," I wanted to say, but held that cruel thought. What would I do if he left me? Was I really paranoid?

When he was asleep, I slipped out of the room and found a phone in the common area and tried calling home. Manu would have reassured me, but no one answered. I went back to the room and slid down inside my cold silk duvet, but my eyes wouldn't close. This duvet was one thing I could thank Paul for however. If he had not insisted on me buying it, I would have had to sleep in the hotel's crummy sheets. I listened to the cockroaches in a corner of the room and later heard Paul get up to use the toilet. Repeatedly. I felt bad for him.

It was the middle of the afternoon when we found ourselves in the heart of Sukhotai, a town further north. It was noisy and chaotic—hard to believe it translated as Dawn of Happiness. We were hungry. The snacks we had eaten along the eight-hour journey did not make for a meal. Antsy, we had dropped our bags at the guesthouse fast. Neither of us had checked how much money we were carrying. I now wasn't sure to have enough to buy lunch. I checked my purse and my money pouch around my waist, Paul looked into his socks and the zip-up back pocket of his short, but all we had were a few baht, enough for the ride back to the guesthouse. Paul had left his credit card and traveler's checks in the room.

"Bollocks!" I said. I was trying to replace my French expressions with English ones. Paul laughed—it was the accent.

"*Merde!*" he said and then I was laughing.

The national anthem started playing from the street speakers and everyone paused to pay respect to their king. I smiled—I didn't even know past the second line of The Marseillaise.

Paul helped me jump into the back of a truck that was supposed to take us back to the hostel. Unlike me, he had this amazing quality of quickly forgiving and moving on from our arguments. I had to pretend everything was good and push my feelings down. I didn't enjoy doing it but I didn't know any other way. We stopped on the side of the road to pick up a monk, who was offered a seat up front, next to the driver. I thought we had the best seat at the back though: in a closed off car, I wouldn't have been able to see or hear a third of what I could from my spot. I would not have seen that woman bargaining in the street with her baby rolled up in a cloth tied to her back, sound asleep amidst all the noise. I would not have noticed all the shades of yellow and orange of the monks' robes that popped out against the faded barracks, like poppies in a field. I would not have smelled the pungent Tiger Balm that the locals rubbed around their nostrils. I would not have pinched my nose when confronted with rancid smells of fish and chicken and I would not have been disgusted by all the people who spat constantly. The best way to meet people was to use the cheapest form of transport. Being in a taxi would have been like covering the city and its people with a giant glass bell, sterilized of all senses.

An old lady sat in the back of the truck with us. Her arms were wrapped around a wicker basket on her lap. It was filled with oranges. We must have been hungrily looking at those oranges because she picked up one of the blessed fruits and handed it to us. We thanked her with the best *kapunka* we had and repeated it once more as it was the only word we knew. *Kapunka* for me and *kapunkap* for Paul. Here was someone with so little, yet she gave so much. No one in the truck spoke English and by the time we realized that we were heading in the wrong direction, I was never more certain that I was in the right place.

The Thais had an expression they frequently used with tourists, especially when trying to sell something: "same-same but different". They would tirelessly try to show the ways in which something was the same while conceding that it was different, which, to them, was a good selling point. The old lady's orange offering made me consider the expression in a different way: we were all different, but same-same.

Chapter 10

I hang up and light another cigarette. Andrew called to say he was coming. The cold air has sobered me. I recognize his silhouette walking down Broadway, tall and proud.

"You're shivering, babe." He covers my shoulders with his jacket and rubs my arms briskly. I apologize. I didn't mean to scream.

"What's happening?"

"Do you have time?" His hands fan open in question mode. "We never have time to talk."

"I'm here," he says. "I'm listening." Andrew reaches for my hand. "Aren't you happy with me? I do my best to make you happy and to provide for us, but that doesn't seem to be enough for you."

"I don't need you to *provide* for me. I have my own money."

He pauses. "What do you need from me?"

I feel tears swelling in my eyes. "I'm taking every job I can get booked for. You work late every day, you even go back to the office on Sundays and now you're going to spend Christmas working in Japan. I know we said we'd work as hard as we could now and save so we can eventually have a family, but what is the point of it all if we're not spending any quality time together? It's like building a high rise on sand." My blood's boiling again. "You had promised me Christmas."

"I truly am sorry, babe, but I have to be there."

I shake my head. "It's your choice in the end."

"No, it's not my fucking choice!" Two passers-by turn around to stare at us. "It won't always be like this," he resumes, in a gentler tone.

I cross my arms around my waist. "I told you it was important for me to spend this holiday with you and my family."

"I know." He takes my free hand. "I don't want to lose you, Coline." He gently squeezes my hand. "My parents fought all the time–I don't want us to fight."

Chapter 11

The hill was steep and my leg muscles were on fire. Paul had expressed concern for me when we booked the trip in Chang Mai, designated for "advanced" hikers, but I ignored him; it was hard to trust anything he said after lying to me about Christy. The physical pain brought out all the anger I felt inside. Bamboo leaves and branches slapped me in the face and scraped my bare legs. I had drunk all my water and felt dizzy. Paul did not turn back to check on me. I wanted to hit him. I wanted him to admit to his lie, beg for forgiveness and then kiss me. I needed some water. I found myself loving and hating Paul at the same time. I kept seeing the email I had read over his shoulder at the Internet café the day before. I had not meant to read it but it mentioned Christy. His friend was teasing him about her–they had dated. When I confronted Paul, he yelled at me and said that I hadn't even read it right.

My foot hit a rock and I almost tripped. I caught myself with one hand against the root of a Banyan tree. Andreja, a Slovenian lady who was walking behind me, helped me get up. I pretended that nothing hurt. She called out for a break to Moh, our leader. "I'm tired too," Andreja said in solidarity. We had been hiking for three hours on rocky ground when we made our first stop in an isolated village. I refilled my water bottle and cleaned the wound on my hand. It was superficial. How long and how far could Paul and I continue on with so little love? We hadn't even had sex since our trip to Kho Chang. I took shelter in the shade of a bamboo canopy. Moh, Andreja and a few others were there, resting. I drank the water, devoured a pear and a cereal bar. My mind quieted down. We were still very far from the village where we were to camp, but the rest of the trek was going to be easier, Moh said.

Children and women gathered to sell their handiwork. They were carrying silver trays of colorful embroideries and jewelry. I let them put bracelets on my wrist. Their touch felt warm. They had belts too. I thought of Mum's wicker basket on top of her dresser. That was where she kept her nice belts. Occasionally, she would let Manu and me pick one to wear to school. I would always borrow the same one: brown suede with white embroidery. I liked the feel of it.

"Bang!" Moh was playing with a rocket bamboo stick. Two kids stood behind, imitating the gesture. The stick was hollow and sounded like a rocket when banged against Moh's thigh. Paul wasn't far, taking pictures. "This is what I used to play with when I was a kid," Moh said. "Hold it by your side, make a fist and tap it against your leg."

One of the women smiled at me. I was taken aback. Her mouth was vermillion red, almost black–it looked like blood. Andreja explained that women from the Lesor tribe chewed Betel nuts to make their teeth and gum red because it was considered beautiful there. A young girl sat next to me and we engaged in a conversation in which we could only guess the meaning of the words. She had thick dark hair, tightly braided, her ears were pierced with over-sized earrings and her wrists were covered with shiny metal bracelets. Her teeth were very white. Moh explained that the tradition was changing because of the tourists' presence in the village.

We resumed our march. Moh led us through lush jungle up into the mountains, but the terrain was easier this time—he'd told the truth. How was I going to forgive Paul if he would not admit he'd lied and ask to be forgiven? I almost tripped again. I slowed my breath and looked ahead, at the moss that had webbed itself between trunk and branches, the waterfalls rippling themselves to infinity in the river and the sunlight revealing the magic of the rolling mountains through the filtering clouds. No camera in the world could capture the beauty of this place. Moh talked about the tribes that came from bordering countries and took refuge in Thailand. If they were lucky, the government let them occupy the land they found in the mountains, but they never got Thai citizenship, not even after fifty years. I felt lucky to be born where I was. I did not have to live in fear that one day I could be deported.

The sun was setting when we reached the village. I wanted Manu to be there. I thought of her photograph tucked in my notebook but her presence was already fading. Behind a shack, women were preparing a curry, sitting on their heels and chatting. Under the stilted houses, kids were chasing chickens, while pigs grunted. I liked that; we were not disrupting anyone's life.

No one needed help and I used my time to go write in my notebook. I settled my backpack in the hut, against the wall made of bamboo poles, and sat against it. My traveling journal, meant to document all I had seen, had turned into a diary. I didn't mean for it to be that way but writing about my fears and other emotions, was the only thing that helped deal with the realities of the adventure. Paul came in to drop his bag next to mine a little later. He left with both cameras around his neck and two extra rolls of film shoved in his pockets. He liked being able to play with both the manual and the digital: one was instant gratification and the other one offered more later. Through the door I saw the evening light, worthy of a Bastille Day fireworks display in France. I placed my journal back in my bag and went outside.

Andreja sat next to me at dinner. Paul was on my right, but we had not made peace yet. Slovenia was a safe little country with mountains, Andreja said. Her job at the committee of Agriculture led her to work with international representatives all the time. She complained only about one aspect of her job: most French texts were not translated into English. All the other ones were. I had no explanation. The conversation naturally moved to nationalities and the differences between countries, as it often did amongst backpackers. It was hard not to generalize. "I met some Parisians and, if you don't mind me asking, why don't the French in general like Americans?"

I did not know what to answer. Each time I tried to articulate a thought, it stopped making sense. All I could see was that thanks to a common language—English—a group of international travelers could meet on a land foreign to each of them and share their worldviews, hopes and dreams. As if the knowledge of the world had been laid out in the construction of a giant prism puzzle, I was learning about my homeland through the eyes of other foreigners. Every one's opinion was being held accountable as one of the many assembling parts needed to form the truth. The world was larger than I had thought—it was dimensional.

I had a lot more to learn if I wanted to teach, I thought.

Moh and his friend, the village chief, put on the table some cut pineapple and watermelon for dessert. I reached for the melon. Paul looked at me and smiled. "Not trusting pineapple anymore?" I shook my head "no". He took a piece of pineapple and bit into it. He offered me the rest of the piece. "I promise, it's just sweet." I ate it. Not a hint of spice. He squeezed my hand underneath the table.

"A shooting star!" someone said.

"Don't point at it!" Moh warned. "It's bad luck. If a woman is pregnant, she will give birth to a duck." I suppressed a laugh.

It was pitch dark and the cold of night had settled at the table. After dinner, the kids emerged from their hut in costume, the women pushing the shy ones forward. Everyone was laughing gently, children included. We left the table to form a half-circle around the bonfire while the kids stood in front of us. They performed their traditional dances with elegance; the graceful movements of their hands and fingers captivated me. Mothers and fathers stood proudly around and everyone clapped. A little girl came nearer. Her hands covered her face, but I could see she was smiling. Her beautiful ebony eyes were sparkling in the light of the fire. I wanted to take her in my arms and sit her on my lap.

"I think she wants you to come dance with her," Paul said.

I took her hand and we joined the circle. I felt like I had elephant feet but she taught me the steps with patience and humor. Children were teachers too. Just hours ago, this little girl and I were strangers—now we were holding hands. We danced until it was time to go to bed.

Lying next to me on the bamboo floor that we shared with the group, Paul took out the digital camera and showed me the pictures he had taken during the evening: the jungle fringing the village, the children dancing in blurry surroundings, the women chatting and Moh and his friend staring at the fields, backlit. His photos were as beautiful as those in the National Geographic magazines he collected. Paul bit his lower lip, turned his camera off and said, "Good night, sweetheart," before rolling over.

I closed my eyes and listened to the silence outside.

Chapter 12

Paul took a few laps by himself in front of the rental store in Pai, revving the engine of the small red motorbike.

"I wish I knew how to ride," I said.

"I'll teach you later, when we're in the countryside. It's not hard. C'mon now." I jumped on behind him. "Are you fine without a helmet?"

I wrapped my arms around him. "I don't need one."

"There's a bar you can hold onto at the back," he shouted in the wind. "When you feel more confident..." I took the challenge and put one hand on the bar. We zoomed away from the quiet little town near the border with Myanmar and up a dirt road into the mysterious mountains before us. The fog heaved itself up and dissipated, revealing luscious green hills, waterfalls and hot springs. Pai was a treasure of a place, with peace and beauty in equal measure. I hoped no developers would come and ruin the landscape. I took my other hand from around Paul's waist and held on tight to the bar at my back.

When we reached a clearing, a flat piece of land dotted with coconut trees, we stopped. "Ready?" Paul said. He explained how a motorbike worked and insisted I forget about the reflexes that came with driving a car. Nervously, I slowly spluttered forward. What had he told me about the brakes? "You're doing great, sweetheart!" I relaxed a little and went faster on longer stretches. "Careful!" There was a tree in front of me. It got close. I kept pressing on the right handlebar. I was forgetting about everything he had said. The tree kept coming. "Brake!" I was trying. "Coline! Brake!" Too late—the motorbike made it halfway up the tree before we crashed to the ground. My chin was torn and the palm of my hand bled a little. Paul humored me at first and then pulled the safety kit he kept in his backpack and helped me clean my wounds. I was too upset to talk. I wanted to prove to him and myself that I could take charge and had completely failed. He got the bike up and we got back on it, Paul in charge and me, along for the ride.

A few hours later, we were lost. We rode up and down the one dirt road of a deserted hamlet to find a sign, but there was nothing except a shop with an old, shabby door. We parked the bike sideways in front of it.

"Hello?" I called. We waited and called out again. A little hunched old man came out of a house adjacent to the shop. He said something in Thai and smiled. There wasn't a tooth left in his mouth. I didn't think he'd be of much help to find our way back.

"Sohadika," Paul and I said in unison. We bowed and pressed our palms together. I pressed mine very lightly—the cut was burning. The old man motioned us inside. Cotton fabrics in earthy shades were hanging on carved wooden sticks pinned to the walls. An old loom sat in the middle of the room with threads tied to a weaving in progress.

I pointed at a brown scarf with an irregular pattern of very thin white stripes running along in the middle. The man rubbed his fingers together, telling me I could touch it. It felt rough in places and soft in others–I liked it. He pressed his hand on my forearm. His eyes shone like pearls against the darkness of his skin, and despite all the wrinkles that were creasing his face it was easy to see that he had once been a very handsome man. He reminded me of my grandfather, Pépé. The old man motioned for me to follow him to the backyard. Paul trailed, his film camera around his neck.

The backyard was small, filled with sticks and herbs. I squatted down next to the old man. He picked up a cotton flower from a patch and reached for my hand. He looked at the wound on my hand quizzically and I imitated a motorbike and a fall. He laughed. I was wrong, there were two teeth left in his mouth. He placed the cotton flower inside my hand and again rubbed his fingers together for me to touch it. I could hear the clicks of Paul's camera. The man paid no attention to Paul. The fluffy flower, just like the scarf inside, was made of those two opposite textures I had felt earlier, both rough and smooth. The ball enveloped a little seed. It was for me to keep, the man said in his language. I emptied my pack of tissues to put the cotton ball in but instead, the man pinched some clay, red like tennis courts, and put it in the small plastic wrapping. His mumbling sounded like a chant. Again I thought of Pépé. He didn't talk much either. When we were little, he would take Manu and me through the farm to see the pigs, ducks and rabbits and we'd walk down to the big field to the sheep that he sheared himself. They looked really funny, bald all over. When Pépé smiled, I saw all his strong white teeth.

With my new treasures secured in the plastic bag, we returned to the shop. I pulled out a few hundred baht from my wallet to purchase the earth-toned scarf he had made.

He tied it around my neck and we bowed goodbye. Outside, Paul revved the engine and I climbed on the back of the motorbike. Hair in the wind, floating between hopes and memories, I didn't care where I was going. Paul squeezed my knee and I knew he was happy for me.

Something shifted for me during that encounter. Even though Paul was with us, it was my adventure. I had connected with someone like I rarely had the opportunity to and felt a sense of peace and control. It was as if I were discovering just who I really was, or who I could be, just as I was discovering new sides to Paul. There was still a part of him that I knew from London, the adventurous, artistic, happy and caring Paul I had fallen in love with, but there was also this other side of him, the side that would get grumpy, ignore me when I took too much of his space and that could even lie and flirt with other girls and make me jealous.

Backpacking was much more than *seeing* new places and yet what we saw was the most recurrent question family, friends and other travelers asked about. It was difficult to identify and understand what I was feeling about myself and about Paul without being able to talk to someone about it. We'd only been traveling for one month and I was as excited as scared for the journey ahead of me.

"Dear God or Buddha, please save us," I prayed in silence. Paul took my hand. He had not touched his cameras hidden away in his bag.

Men with Kalashnikovs had been getting on and off our bus for the last three hours. Every time we stopped to let one in or out, I readied myself to be called up from the back, brought to the front and shot in the middle of the forehead.

Paul's placid expression told me how worried he was; he'd stopped reading and listening to music a long time ago.

"We'll be fine, sweetheart," he said. "I don't think it's about us. They're looking for someone." He was chewing on the skin around his fingernails.

We had left Thailand a week earlier for Laos. We relaxed for a few days in a nice guesthouse in Luang Prabang and made plans to head up to the Plain of Jars when a young American man ran into us one night in the staircase. He had his backpack on and was yelling to everyone who would listen not to take Route 13. Route 13 was the only road that went to Phonsavan, the Plain of Jars, or anywhere else for that matter. He said he was going back to Thailand, which was what the American Embassy recommended on their website. We thought they were exaggerating the danger. Besides, we weren't about to backtrack.

No one on the bus spoke English. We didn't know if the men were soldiers or Hmong rebels. We didn't know anything. Taking so much risk to see some mysterious jars—some funeral urns, storage or big cooking pots—the guidebook wasn't even clear about. When scientists knew how to launch a rocket on another planet, when doctors could re-attach an arm to a body, I found it fascinating that no one could agree on what a collection of old pottery was used for. The bus slowed as we passed an overturned bus on the side of the road: it was blackened and still smoking. One man in a khaki shirt and pants asked to stop after we had passed the scene when he saw armed men lined up along Route 13. He got off to chat with them. I urgently needed a toilet. I had been holding on for hours, hoping for a real toilet but instead there had been two breaks where only men could go pee beside the road, their back to the bus. I couldn't squat on the open road in front of men–armed men. The rocky road was making my condition worse. I thought I would go at the next stop, even if that meant doing it in front of everyone, but with a bus burning, I reconsidered my options.

Days before, we were racing down the Mekong River at sixty kilometers an hour in a speedboat. I felt crazily alive. I had celebrated the unknown. But here I was now, ready to pee in my pants. I thought of the brief conversation I had had with Manu on a crackly phone line in Pai and wondered if that was the last one we'd have.

Two people boarded the bus–a woman who was carrying lots of plastic bags, sat at the front of the bus and a man who sat opposite her. The man in the khaki shirt got back on. If the men with the guns had wanted to kill us–the few Westerners that were on the bus–they would have surely done it by now. But just as I started to relax, I heard one traveler tell his companion the story of two tourists on a motorbike who got hacked to death with axes just days earlier.

We were close to the Plain of Jars. The roads were bare. It looked like a war zone. The consequences of the Vietnam War had extended far beyond the country's geographical limits and Laos had been brutally, heavily bombed. We could see more signs as we got closer to town. One of them portrayed happy kids holding hands. On the next one, they went to play in a field. And on the last one, very sad kids were missing arms and legs and blood was spurting from their wounds. There was no need to speak any particular language to get the message.

We reached the small town center and the bus came to a final stop. Leaving my backpack behind on the roof of the bus, I ran to the first café I saw.

Paul and I settled in a guesthouse that had mortar shells for flowerpots. We met two other backpackers and made plans to have dinner that night but first I wanted to call home. I needed familiar voices to fill my heart. Mum picked up the phone. A shot of adrenaline came rushing to my heart at the sound of her voice. It wasn't her usual tone. "Is it Dad?" I asked.

"Yes," she said weakly, "he's in hospital."

I bombarded her with questions. He had had a heart attack. He had been in intensive care for two weeks while I was ambling around aimlessly. I could–should–have been with him. I pushed down the tears that were welling up fast. My throat tightened.

"Why didn't you tell me sooner?" I cried.

"I'm telling you now," Mum said.

"I leave home and then that's it, I'm not included anymore, like I'm no longer part of the family?" My voice quivered. My credit was running out faster than I could put coins in the machine and I grabbed some from Paul who was on the other phone.

"You're being unfair, Coline. He didn't want you to be worried. You need to understand: it was his decision and we had to respect it. I can't stay on the phone, darling, I'm sorry. I was just leaving for the hospital. Don't worry. He's fine now. Call me tomorrow and soon you'll be able to talk to him, ok?"

I had to be tough. "Ok."

"Are things good with Paul?"

I had to be tough. "Yes, it's… all good."

"I love you, honey. Don't worry. Things are going to be ok."

She hung up before me, which she never did. My stomach cramped. I stepped out of the phone booth, unwilling to cry in front of Paul who had also finished his conversation with his mum. He had seen me cry enough already.

"Are you ok, sweetheart?" He put out his cigarette and stretched his arms open to pull me in an embrace. I pulled away.

"Dad is in the hospital."

"What?" He hesitated. I was not moving. "Come here–"

"No, it's fine. I'm fine. Everybody's fine, just like you say."

"Sweetheart…"

"You know what? Actually, it's not fucking fine!" I stood in the middle of the pavement, stunned. The tears I was pushing away were burning. "It's been two weeks and I didn't know. I should be with him right now. I should call the airline and leave as soon as possible."

"Let's think about it tonight and discuss it in the morning before rushing into any decision, don't you think?"

"Can I have a cigarette?" He pulled one out from his pack and lit it for me. I took one long deep drag. "They didn't tell me anything. They kept it secret. I feel… betrayed!" Paul made another attempt to hold me, but I backed off again. "You don't even care about me anymore."

"What? What are you talking about? That's not true and you know it."

"Why don't you want to have sex with me anymore, then?"

"Coline–calm down."

"Why?" My stare was defiant.

"I do, sweetheart. Just not when we quarrel so much."

"If you did not lie to me, we wouldn't "quarrel" so much, whatever that means."

"We argue a lot. But you misunderstood that email."

"Oh really?"

Paul drew closer. "Listen to me. I've never cheated on you, nor am I lying to you. I love you." He forced me into a hug. I was too numb to hug back or push away. "Let's go for dinner. We need a meal after whatever that was today."

I followed Paul to the café where the couple we had met had ordered pizzas. I barely registered my surroundings. Dad could have been dead and I wouldn't even have known. Was I not a member of the family anymore? Paul and now them… I really was on my own. This was not how I had imagined our trip. I took a slice, mechanically, and drank, mechanically. Images were swirling in my mind: men with Kalashnikovs, children stepping on mines, and Dad on a hospital bed without any news from his traveling daughter.

"I can't wait to get to Vang Vieng," the Australian guy said. "Magic pizza, tubing down the river… It's gonna be awesome!"

Paul laughed, sipped and ate as if everything were normal. He asked the backpackers if they knew anything about the bus incident on Route 13. An officer had been shot dead and some angry farmers had burnt down a bus to protest against the mayor's speech earlier that morning. The soldiers were there to protect us against the rebels, they said. The Australians ordered another round of Beerlao. The sun dropped and hid behind the dark blue mountains and the colors in the sky faded. I stared at the flowerpots and barbecues made of scrap metal from the war. It was our entire fault: we had planted these mines and we had left them there to kill people years later. I had always thought that we were "the good guys" and that revolutionaries, or "rebels" in other countries were "the bad ones". I thought about the wars we created believing we were saving people, while killing others… Maybe those we called enemies in our countries were not on the wrong side of the trail and maybe they were just hungry, like the farmers who had burnt down the bus on Route 13.

My sleep was restless that night. Should I stay and keep traveling or leave to be with my family? I did not know what to do. Paul had set his alarm clock for six a.m. An early bus was going to take us to the Plain of Jars. Dad didn't want me to stop traveling—I had to respect that.

A kick on the side of the bus sent a clanking vibration to my seat. I turned the key in the ignition again and again. Nothing. The bus wouldn't start. If I stayed here I was going to get hit. The men outside broke a window. Hurry! I ordered myself. The bus shook. One of the men hacked at the bus with a machete. I'd be next. Come on! Start! An explosion, glass everywhere, the bus door shattered. They were going to kill me.

I woke up with a bomb inside my heart. Did we just have an accident or was I having a heart attack? I sat up and looked around the bus. Paul was sleeping one row ahead, his face leaning against the window. My heartbeat slowed down. It was just a nightmare. *Clank-clank-clank.* But *this* was real. *This* was the bus driver killing the gearshift. I leaned into the aisle and watched the driver murdering the transmission, hearing, feeling metal jamming against metal. I couldn't wait to leave Laos. It was now midnight and we hadn't yet crossed the border into Vietnam. A rancid smell of fish hit me. An old man shifted in his seat, cleared his throat with a scraping racket and spat thick phlegm out the window. Repulsed, I rubbed some Tiger Balm around my nostrils to cover the smell. Hard to believe that neither the noise nor the smell had woken Paul up. For once, we were not packed like sardines—there was plenty of room to stretch out. We had about eleven hours of traveling ahead of us. The light was too dim to read or write and the batteries for my CD player had died. I closed my eyes hoping to drift back to sleep but the men with machetes were still haunting me.

Clank-clank-clank. We came to a fork in the road and the driver made a sharp right. There were no signs. How did he know?

I needed guidance. Since my last year in high school, I had found my calling. My junior years had been a struggle— bullied for being tall and skinny, and in shock after the death of my cousin and grand-pa, but inspired by my mum and my English teacher I realized that I too wanted to work with kids. I could help them go through those difficult years, be there to push the door open for conversation, support and encouragement. I knew what I wanted to do. I was safe. But since we had been on the road, Paul and I, crossing so many different lives and possibilities, I doubted myself. What if I weren't a good teacher?

Claaaank. The bus came to a stop. Paul moved but did not wake up. I stared out the window. We were nowhere. Where were we going together if I could not trust him? I missed the simplicity of my life in England. I missed Friday night's fish and chips watching Graham Norton on TV at Paul's place and the long Saturday morning of cuddling in bed, followed by Sunday roast dinner at his parents. However short that time was, I felt safe there with him.

Paul woke up slowly. He got up and I made space next to me. "What's happening?"

"Mechanical problem," I said. "I think the clutch finally gave up." It meant hours of waiting around. We were getting used to those "mechanical problems."

We sat on the side of the deserted road for nearly three hours while the driver worked on the engine. Finally, haltingly, noisily, we pulled back onto the road and drove on as desolate plains stretched before us.

"We're getting close to the border," Paul said and pointed at the guards by the side of the road. He picked up his camera and changed seats to get a better angle. I stayed where I was to watch the sunrise, big like an orange.

Chapter 13

A small package is waiting in front of the door when I come home from upstate New York. Sarah and I hiked Breakneck Ridge Trail this morning and went apple picking in the afternoon. She dropped me in front of my building and drove off, home to Brooklyn. I scoop the package up and head for the kitchen with my bounty from the farm: apples, pumpkins and a jar of raw honey. Andrew is not home. I resist the urge to pour myself a glass of wine and light a cigarette. I open the bubbled envelope instead–a notebook with a note Mum slipped inside. "Ma chérie, I was vacuuming under your bed this morning and I stumbled upon all your travel notebooks from the year you went backpacking with Paul. I thought that maybe it would help you to write again." I told Mum about the doubts I've been having about–well, everything, lately. How much I miss her right now.

On the ride back from Cold Spring, Upstate, the agent from my agency's acting division called to give me details about an audition for tomorrow–a small role in an indie movie. When I practiced the lines with Sarah I sounded awful. I'll make a fool of myself at the audition, I said. Sarah suggested I take some acting classes but I am too scared to try. I spend the evening memorizing my part so I only make a half-fool of myself.

Andrew texts me back as I'm getting into bed. He's out with some clients and says he'll be back late. I open the notebook Mum sent and start writing. I stop to read my rambling on the page, tear it off and shut the light.

Sitting on the kitchen bench, still in my pajamas, I dip a spoon into the small honey jar, lick half of it off and let the rest of the nectar melt in a steaming cup of tea. My throat has been sore since the farm visit last week, and I've polished off most of the jar. The three pumpkins on the kitchen counter are glowing. Andrew walks out of the bedroom buttoning his shirt, a stiff white cotton fabric with thin blue stripes.

"Do you want to see a play with me tonight?" I ask. Outside, the wind spins loudly around the building.

"I'm taking a client out tonight," Andrew says. He knots his tie in front of the hallway mirror. I want to say "again?" but bite my tongue. He's had meetings almost every day and every night this month. "Since when do you go to the theatre, anyway?"

"Since Steven sent me on an audition last week." I haven't heard back from them, but I actually had fun reading the lines. Mum used to take us see the classics: Molière, Racine, Corneille. I miss that. Andrew looks at his smartphone and answers an email. I send Sarah a text to see if she wants to go out with me tonight. Andrew is ready to walk out. "Hey," I say.

"I've got to run. Sorry. Bye, babe." He walks out without giving me a kiss—an infringement to the rule we have agreed on.

The windows shake.

I get my notebook from my sock drawer and settle in the sofa with my cup of tea. Traffic noise is carried up on the wind. Some days New York seems to be only a small town, an isolated island where you can know a lot of people and other times, it feels so big it makes me feel insignificant. My phone vibrates on the coffee table–Sarah is on for tonight. I type in the details about the play when my phone vibrates again. It's Andrew this time. "Sorry about earlier. I'm really stressed out. Let's have dinner tomorrow night and make plans for New Year's Eve." I don't answer and get ready for my castings.

I wake up in a sweat from a nightmare. The play I saw tonight with Sarah–the story of a woman abused in her childhood by her uncle–disturbed me. Andrew isn't back. It's 4 a.m. I get up and find him asleep on the sofa–again. He says only watching TV relaxes him after a stressful day at work, and because I refuse to have a screen in the bedroom, he's now been falling asleep on the couch more and more. The smell of whisky hangs in the air. It's sickening. The moon shines through the window, full like a balloon. It's cold and drizzling out. I go back to bed. I pick up my notebook again and take fast notes of the words and images running through my mind.

Anger
He's chasing me
Anger
What is it?
Anger
I don't know, I'm scared
Anger

I'm not angry
No?
No
Why is someone chasing you?
I don't know
Anger
Do you think I'm bad?
Anxiety
You're sweating, you're twisting
I'm—
What am I?
You're running after something
No. Someone is running after me
I can feel it
In your guts
Your kidney
Your scar
Your spasms
Your liver
Your heat and coldness
Your C4 vertebra
The tension in your thighs
You're resisting
You want to move
Yes
I am trapped
Paralyzed
Tied to the table
My thighs spread out
The baby is crying
Let me go
Love me

Don't leave me
Take me
Free me
Love me
Save me

This makes no sense. I turn off the light and cry silently in bed. This is not the life I had dreamt of. Where did I get lost—when? I thought I wanted to settle down and start a family—I thought it would make me feel loved and safe. I thought having money would make us both stress-free and happy, but the more riches we strive for, the more worried and disconnected we are. There's more to lose now and less and less space for love, and less happiness. It's absurd.

Chapter 14

Tut!!! *Tut, tut, tut, tut, tut!!!!*

"How are we going to cross?" I asked Paul. "It's impossible!"

"Miss!" someone yelled. I turned my head and men started waving at me from every direction. *Tut, tut-tut* "Taxi?" *Tut* "Hello, motorbike?" *Tut-tut.*

"Paul!"

"Miss! Miss!"

"Don't look," Paul said, "just go." He stepped in front of me.

With pavements reserved for street vendors and motorbikes to park, honking, buzzing and head twisting was de rigueur in Hanoi, the so-called Paris of the East. To my right, swarms of motorbikes were coming at me like hungry mosquitoes. I couldn't see Paul anymore. I looked for a green or red light, but couldn't see any. Paul was already on the other side of the road. How had he managed that? I closed my eyes for an instant. Paul called me from the other side and I slowly started walking through the craziness unfolding with every step I took, bikes and motorbikes swerving around me in utter disorder.

"Just keep walking," Paul yelled.

Because there was no other choice and Paul was pressing me, I looked straight in front of me and kept walking. I expected a bike to hit me at any moment, but it didn't happen. I threw myself fully in the water and surfed on the wave that pushed me safely to the other side of the street without a scrape.

"See, you're fine," Paul said, eyes on his guidebook.

I threw him a dark look that he didn't notice.

At the latest backpacker hostel we booked a trek to Sapa, a small town at the northern part of the country, close to the Chinese border. We were to leave that night for the mountains. I was glad I had packed my fleece jacket despite Paul making fun of me in London. Now he had to go shopping for one. The streets of Hanoi were mine for an hour. The cafés with small round tables on the terrace reminded me of France. I walked into a bistro with large open doors and windows. Massive mirrors hung from the walls, tired from the old yellow paint on their backs. I took a seat next to a carved wooden column facing the street, ordered a lemonade and opened up my diary. It was perfect.

A couple of tables away, a man was staring at me. His white hair was sleekly brushed over the balding center of his head, a white vest was tucked into his shorts, matching his white knee-high socks in his open-toe sandals. A glass of ice tea was sitting in front of him.

"Where are you from?" he asked.

"France."

"Ha, so we can speak French then!" He broke into a big warm smile and moved his chair closer to mine. "I'm Fred." We shook hands. I could tell from the accent that Fred was Swiss, French Swiss. "I was a Para in the legion," he said without much further introduction. "I fought in Dien Bien Phu. Maybe you're too young to know. That was 1954."

He leant on his forearms over his table and narrowed his eyes a few times, and they seemed to turn a darker shade of blue.

"We lost thirty thousand men in only fifteen days." He coughed a couple of times. "I watched my friends die." I kept silent and only sipped my lemonade when he sipped his tea. "Oh, war is something. They had AA guns…"

"What's AA?"

"Anti-aircraft."

I didn't know what that meant but I didn't want him to stop talking. Fred made me hear the gunshots, smell the hot grenades, see the battlefields filled with lifeless young men and I almost tasted blood. He painted the color of the places and faces he knew as if it had been yesterday. His lips contorted and his eyes widened at times. His voice remained firm and soft at the same time. Sadness never seemed to have left him. I could sense a certain helplessness. He reclined in his chair, extended his legs and took a few more sips of his iced tea while watching people pass by in the street.

"I don't know how I got out of it alive." He was leaning forward again. "I don't know how I survived Alger too."

One man, two wars. How was that possible?

He saluted a man passing outside and continued. "There were bombings everywhere in the country. The worst were the Americans. Their weapons were horrible. Poison gas— you should see what that does."

All those images of Chernobyl that I had seen in schoolbooks or at The Memorial museum in Caen rushed to my mind.

"That's why Americans were treated so badly in the prisons. I think there are still some hiding in the jungle."

"And you? Were you a prisoner?"

"Me? Yes, but not for long. And the Vietnamese were ok with me there. They've always been nice to me. That's why I came back to live here. I love them." He nodded to another man passing by, got a smile back on his face and made a gesture towards the street. "Did you see those guys on motorbikes? They're acrobats, aren't they?" He laughed. His light blue eyes were sparkling again.

Fred finished his tea, saluted me and left. I looked at the time, packed my notebook and met Paul where we had agreed on.

Two days later, Paul and I stepped onto the platform at the station in Lao Cai. We had taken an overnight train from Hanoi and were still an hour away from Sapa. It was 6 a.m. and I was freezing. Paul got us two coffees from a man crouched on the ground. The morning mist was blurring the horizon but I could still see the mountains sprinkled with a touch of snow. I rolled my scarf twice around my neck and put on a few more layers—it was all of my clothing. A Christmas feeling settled inside of me as we crossed the decorated station to the bus terminal. The bus to Sapa was leaving soon and we made it onboard with a minute to spare. In London, that holiday feeling would have come weeks ago with the street ornaments, the school Christmas lunch and the tree in Paul's living room, reaching up to the low ceiling, waiting for me to decorate it with him. I had spent more time at his place than at mine. I missed the peace we had found together there, the laundry tumbling loud in the machine, covering the sound of TV in the living room, watching Paul cook with Nina Simone on, candles lit atop the fireplace, sitting on the carpet, comment on his photography books... There was no more romance to the way we were traveling and I missed it terribly. Loving Paul was so easy then. "I love you and I want to be with you," I could still hear him say. We say those words too rarely, as if there was a finite amount of them.

A crowd of clamoring children came running towards us when we arrived in the village an hour later. Girls from the Flower H'mong tribe greeted us with smiley faces. How could they keep warm in skirts and wool socks pulled up to their knees? A little girl stretched her arm out to show me the beautiful bracelets she had made, while, next to her, a tall girl was showing us a hand-sewn bed cover.

Paul climbed up on the roof of the bus and jumped down with his heavy bag resting on one shoulder, and mine on the other. I stared, suddenly so attracted to him. A boy with a thick black fringe across his forehead offered to clean Paul's shoes. Paul simply laughed and explained to the boy that he couldn't put polish on the kind of boots he was wearing, but that maybe later, he could brush them for him. He always was so open and patient with kids—especially with his brother's. He would have made a great teacher. Following his lead, I told the girls I would first drop my bag and come back to see them once I had settled in.

The hotel gave us a magnificent room with a view and balcony. Paul opened the window and lit two cigarettes, one for me, one for him. I could see over the whole valley. Thick layers of mist were blending green and dark blue hues together. I breathed in the pure crisp clear air. A cloud was pushing the white silk chiffon away to slowly reveal the blue milky mountains that separated us from the Chinese border. I leant over the balcony. A woman was walking up a quirky street with a load of laundry on one hip. On the far right the little boy who polished shoes was working on a pair of boots.

The center of the village was buzzing with life. It was market day. Local and mountain people had assembled in the shade of the multi-colored canvases that had been tied together above the stalls. Rays of sunlight hit the plastic ceilings brandishing bright blue, red, green and yellow streaks across the aisles. The spice stands were a festival of colors. Paul observed people through his lens and I did so through my every sense. Dry meat, fruits and ginger, incense sticks, bracelets, and wooden bowls were stacked up next to each other in no apparent order. The spicy Tiger Balm was now smelling sweet to me, but I still had to cover my nose when I walked past meat and fish rotting away in the sun, lying on simple pieces of cardboard. Exciting and overwhelming, the market was the beating heart of the village. Vietnamese dialects and broken English, along with donkeys, buses, motorbikes and bells all managed to sing in harmony.

A tribal woman squatting before a large wok tempted me with a chicken dish. I would have had some for lunch if I had not received an email from Mum warning me about the new disease spreading over Europe from Asia, called H5N1, or "Bird flu". They had enough to worry about at home with Dad, without me getting sick in Vietnam. (I suspected that it was Dad's responsibilities at the office that had triggered the heart attack. He worked too many long hours, which did not help Mum's anxious nature.)

We returned to the hotel, where I got myself involved in some unavoidable shopping with the kids—the same ones I had met earlier. I had taken the small habit of turning my ring in, hiding the stones, wherever I felt uncomfortable wearing it. The oldest girl remembered my name and then called me "sister". She threw her arm over my shoulders and together we walked around the main square so she could introduce me to her friends and cousins. They all were such sweet, respectful and hard-working kids, I could see myself spending more time in Sapa with them. I met with Paul in the common area of the hotel where they served a vegetable noodle soup, community-style, and later we walked in the cold and misty night, arm-in-arm. The trek we had booked started early the next day, and it was only 9 p.m. when we went to bed. It was a king size bed with nice clean sheets and covers. I caved against Paul and slowly, tenderly, our bodies warmed up against each other.

The climb was steep but felt effortless. I had developed some fitness and strengthened my leg muscles. The montagnards, the local mountain people, walked up and down the road carrying heavy loads at the same pace as us. Their skin was blue from dying their clothes with the Indigo flower.

We had been walking uphill through glistening paddy fields for a while, when I noticed a little boy was following us. He was barefoot. He played shy for a while. When we broke for lunch, he came around. His face and hands were covered with mud and one of his front teeth was chipped. Paul picked up his digital camera and went to sit with the boy on a big rock, where they took turns taking pictures of each other. The boy had never seen such a camera. One moment he was kneeling besides Paul, the next, standing over his shoulder— he was ecstatic. When we had gone to Brighton, Paul had brought a spare manual camera to teach me the basic principles of photography. I was that little boy, full of wonder, and I was now falling in love with Paul all over again.

Back in Sapa the next day, where mountains seemed to arise from dark watercolor paintings, Paul and I rented another motorbike. We rode up the Flower River and passed the Cat-Cat waterfall. Water splashed on the rocks and cooled me down, my hair flew in the wind like a kite in the sky and I cheered at the warmth of the sun on the skin of my face. I could have stayed on that motorbike with Paul forever. It was the most free I had ever felt.

We watched the sun set in a myriad of pinks and oranges over the mountains. "I could live here," I said. "I could open a French restaurant or a bakery like the one in town, Baguette et Chocolat." Just like in Koh Chang, it struck me again how little was necessary to be happy. What we didn't need, we didn't miss. Water, mountains, trees, fresh air, and color: I was rich.

Chapter 15

"Sorry babe."

"It happens." We both know work's stressing him. I put on a long woolly sweater over my underwear. Andrew steps into the shower and I go to the living room. He leaves for Japan tomorrow. I would kill for a cigarette. I open the window for a little bit of fresh air. It's warm for an early December evening. On the job today, the stylist quoted the Bible. "We entertain angels unaware," she said. An ambulance passes by—I look for angels on the fire escape. Suicides are on the rise, the journalist announced on TV this morning. People are losing their job by the thousands. Others, perhaps the same ones, are losing their life savings.

I go to the kitchen and make myself a cup of tea with honey.

An air of Normandy drifts in and a low light settles below the charcoal-blue sky. I'm cold now and close the window. Every single object around me is void of emotion, of connection. If I weren't with Andrew, would I actually stay in New York? I came to the city for work, but he's the reason why I stayed.

"Don't you believe in anything?" the stylist asked at work.

"I believe in a lot of things," I told her. "I think something greater exists, whether it's called God, Spirit, or Energy. And

I believe we continuously evolve and adapt, like Nature does." I was aware of the power of her faith. This was the confidence she had when she spoke the phrase about angels that stopped me. I suppose this is how she could go through her husband's death, trusting that there was a higher plan and that he was in a better place. I can't even go through a day without questioning what I am doing in New York, so far away from home, if my job is really making me happy or what is going to happen between Andrew and me.

There now are pills to treat hair-loss in the bathroom cabinet and Ambien tablets on the bedside table. He refuses to engage in any serious conversation about work—it's hard to feel close to him when I feel pushed away.

Something cold slides down my neck and décolleté. Andrew kisses me gently on the ear. "I wanted to wait for Christmas to give it to you, but I'm leaving soon. I want you to have it now." I look down at the diamond on my chest and turn around. He explains that he had it made especially for me in the Diamond District. I fake enthusiasm and kiss him.

"I forgot to tell you. Gary and Laura invited us to St Kitts for the New Year. They rented a huge villa. We'll have a great time." Why do I have the feeling of being manipulated? They're not my favorite friends of his. "I need some sun, babe." It's true. He does need to relax. "Please, say yes." He presses himself against me and I can feel him growing harder. "Have I told you how beautiful you looked?" I want to push him away and pull him closer to me at the same time. He kisses my ears, nibbles on the lobes and licks me down my neck. He mumbles things I can barely hear, removes my sweater and kisses every inch of me. I am split between pleasure and unease—something has to change.

Chapter 16

From mountains to waterfalls, through caves and beaches, Vietnam was full of sacred places. In Nha Trang, a small town by the sea front, Paul suffered another stomach virus. I let him rest and hired a motorbike-driver for the day. I took pictures at leisure: a family of four passing by on a motorbike, men napping in their tuk-tuk and grilled peanuts spread on plastic sheets on the side of the road. I tried some artichoke tea with the driver and his friends and shared lunch with him. I stopped at every temple I wanted to visit and took my time inside, burning incense, lighting candles and inventing prayers so Dad would recover fast and I asked for help to decide what I would do at the end of the trip. There were no clear answers—it would have to come later. That day I did not have to make any compromises. By myself, it was as if there was more time, and less stress.

We reached Ho Chi Minh City, formerly called Saigon during the French presence, a few days later. Since our visit to Laos, I had developed a small obsession with the Vietnam War. The War Remnants Museum retraced the atrocities perpetrated by the US Army on the guerrillas and the Vietnamese civilians. Image after image made me feel sicker and sicker. I couldn't take the pictures of the Napalm-burnt bodies and faces, or the 'frag-bombs' victims. I didn't know why I insisted on looking at this. Was I being morbid, or was it because I wanted to know what had happened to this country—something to explain all the mutilated people begging in the streets? I was aware how what I was seeing was a fragmented picture of the war and its aftermath but I felt this was one of the facets of the prism that no one would have seen in an American movie or museum.

I shared my home in London with four roommates. One of them was from China. One night after watching the news and talking about the Tiananmen massacre, we realized that Cheng had never heard of it. He said he did not believe us and we thought it was a joke at first. Cheng was far from being an ignorant person. His country had forbidden access to certain historical facts, it seemed. The five of us went online—on Chinese websites—and read that no students had died, only criminals. This was insane. I wondered if it was possible that my own country had kept secrets of that sort from us. If they had, maybe it was better that way, I thought at the time. That was stupid, I realized now watching pictures of bodies being dragged across the ground by US Army tanks. One picture in particular of four GIs stood out: a man was holding two heads, one in each hand. He was smiling and so were the soldiers next to him. Two bloody headless bodies lay at their feet.

I had come to this place to get a clearer picture of the war but I was leaving even more confused. What could justify this? How did we manage to reach such inferior levels of humanity? Why all this violence, this degrading violence?

Somehow, I could not blame the soldiers. A song from French artist Jean-Jacques Goldman kept badgering me. With my own translation: *"And if I was born in 17 in Leidenstadt/ On the ruins of a battle field/ Would I have been better or worse than those people/ If I had been German?"* It was easy to apply the questionings about one war to another. Would I have been better or worse than those people if I had been an American soldier? Would I have been smiling too and looking proud of myself if I had been conditioned to fear, hate and kill?

At dinner, Paul ordered some wantons and sweet steamed pork buns. I wanted to throw up. I was sick to my stomach, sick of us, white people always thinking we were better, smarter and more "developed" than other people. Paul didn't understand what I was feeling. I was being too sensitive, he said. Later in bed, he asked me if I wanted to leave for Cambodia the next day. I was relieved to leave earlier.

I recharged, gliding along the Mekong on our way to Cambodia. The river was the lifeblood for its people–a place to wash, to fish and raise ducks. Every second spent watching those people was a photograph. Every minute, a "hello" echoed across the water. Kids waved at us in the boat and I waved back at them. Again, we didn't need to speak the same language to communicate. That kind of beauty could only come from the path found between people's hearts. Children played in the river, unaware how poor they were compared to Western standards, and I quite aware how "rich" I was. On that little flow of happiness, with Paul by my side, I sailed away towards softer skies and the most perfect memory of London's great river, the Thames.

For three months, every Thursday after work, I used to visit Milly. I taught her French. When she would receive me in her home, there always was a tray with two porcelain cups, a teapot and a plate of French biscuits on a small table. We would converse as much as we could *"en français."* I longed all week for Milly's cup of tea and Gavottes—delicious crispy buttery waffles wrapped in gold paper. Her constant progress and motivation made me feel appreciated. When we stopped our conversation at the end of September, she had just started teaching me something she called Positive Thinking. "The way you say something is of great importance," Milly assured me. "If we change the way we speak and get rid of the negative words and phrases, we'll be able to improve our lives." I did not really believe it. I did not know how to change my way of talking, but I had very positive memories of my time with her. The most extraordinary one was her goodbye present. She had invited me to come on her boat. We cruised for a couple of hours, passing bridges and marshes, and I filled my head and heart with the breath of the river, fresh and pungent. We anchored in a small cove, put on thick jumpers and watched the sky fade from bright pink to dark purple. From the cooler box that we had carried from her car to the sailboat, Milly pulled out a lobster. This, to me, was reserved for special occasions like Christmas. And while I screamed with excitement, she produced a bottle of champagne. It was New Year's Eve *and* Christmas all together!

"J'ai préparé une petite picnic," she articulated. I could not hold my tears.

As Paul and I slid along the Mekong, more kids waved hello and I imagined Milly on the other side of the river. I waved and waved and waved, until my wrist grew tired.

The picture faded and morphed a few hours later into a mythological scene. Women dressed in white were balancing themselves, perched on the tip of elongated barks, with a long thin stick in each hand. I could not tell if those beautiful mermaids of the Mekong were rowing or dancing. They pulled and pushed, bent and crisscrossed, with the grace of swans and the strength of Olympic athletes.

The Southeast Asia I had come to experience was layered with moments rendered magical by their simplicity and unexpectedness, and moments of the sad truth about poverty, and sometimes even horror.

When we entered the old Prison S-21 in Phnom Penh, it was like walking through the living nightmare the prisoners had suffered. How could a place of life and joy such as a school, be transformed into a place of torture? Classrooms had been turned into cells of hell. Anyone suspected of opposition to the Khmer regime, along with each of their family members, was sent there, imprisoned, questioned, monstrously tortured, and killed. Some of the executioners were children.

It frightened me to think that we could leave all humanity and civilization behind to regress to this animalistic state, under fear and pressure—how powerful was fear! Was that a survival instinct or had those people actually been born monsters? Again, would I have done the same if I had been there? Those who refused to follow orders were killed. At the backpackers' place that evening, I started reading a book that Paul had picked up about a new society Pol-Pot had tried to create, but I had to stop. It was too violent. I looked for the book I had placed on the library shelves in the morning, but it was gone. Only J. K. Rowling's narrative skills could have pulled me out of my mood. I sat down with my diary and a beer.

If I had questioned the existence of a God before, I lost all hopes at the Killing Fields a few miles outside of Phnom Penh. I stood with Paul in front of a glass tower filled with skulls. "No bullet waste" had been the order given to the guards. Armed with metal bars and bamboo sticks they would beat people and hit babies' head against the trees. From the ground, bone and clothing particles were sticking out. From a tree, a tooth… Somewhere underneath, the parents and brothers of our guide. Behind me, two American women were crying in a heartbreaking leitmotiv: "I can't believe it. I had no idea." I felt their cry deep inside me. There was no God. We were all alone. Nowhere was safe.

In the capital, people with amputated legs and arms used their handicap to beg. We were told not to give money because it encouraged people to hurt their children. I was tormented. Nothing felt normal. A blind man was playing a harmonica, kids were lying on the pavement and old people were staring in the emptiness of the streets. There was now a genocide happening in Sudan. My thoughts played on repeat. I kept feeling guilty. I was born in a rich, peaceful country. I couldn't give money to the beggars and I didn't even know what they really needed.

"You won't leave me?" I asked Paul in bed. I was failing again at being strong. He lowered his book and stared at me, confused. "I'm just scared. The prison. The torture. Everything." I desperately needed him to hold me in his arms and was relieved he did so when I asked him to. He wasn't moved as intensely as I was by The Killing Fields, but he too had been shocked to discover the level of cruelty used by the Khmer Rouge.

"Let's skip the beach," he said, "and head to Australia sooner, if you want." I nodded and relaxed a little. Paul put his book down, and we made love with tenderness.

There was one thing though that we could not miss before leaving Cambodia; we had to visit the site of Siem Reap, where Hindu and Buddhist gods and traditions co-existed in the form of sculptures and engravings.

"You buy him because he is a boy, not fair," a little girl with postcards complained in front of Angkor Wat, the most impressive temple.

Paul had just bought a pack of ten postcards from a little boy.

"You buy me and I leave you alone after," she said. I didn't know what to think about it: was she being smart or demanding?

I followed Vishnu and Apsara, smiling and dancing and let Prince Rama and his monkey's army lead me to one last temple, where a skinny old man offered to read my palms. He promised that 2004-2007 were going to be very good years and that I was going to marry in 2004. There was hope for the years to come.

As we bounced along the road in a noisy old bus on our way to Poipet, a frontier town of Cambodia and Thailand, I foretold that there would be no more bumps on the road, no more broken bridges, but very good flat tarmac by 2020. Maybe.

I was ready to leave.

Goodbye beautiful kids, I whispered through the window on the bus. And once more, hello the unknown.

PART II

Notice that the stiffest tree is most easily cracked, while the bamboo or willow survives by bending with the wind.
—Bruce Lee

Chapter 17

I roll my heavy luggage to my old bedroom under mum's huge smile: the prodigal daughter has returned. I had to pack both warm and light clothes for Normandy and St Kitts.

"I'll let you get settled," Mum says, lingering in the doorway, before returning to the kitchen where Dad's waiting for her instructions.

A part of me feels like a stranger when I come back home; I need to do things that feel familiar immediately. I zip open my luggage, pull out my Christmas gifts, and hide them under the bed like I used to.

The dream-catcher Manu gave me still hangs against my bookshelf at the foot of my bed. When I was little I would tell all my nightmares to my sister during breakfast. She never had any, but sympathized as best she could. The day she left home for college, I didn't know how I'd live without her. Life would forever be lonely. Up until then, Manu had been a daily presence in my life. To comfort me the afternoon she left, Mum said that one day I too would leave. I felt sorry for my parents, but I prayed for my time to come fast. I knew I loved my sister before, but never as much as I did that day she left.

I hear the front door opening again. Manu's home!

I race to the door and grab her hand and pull her to my room where we get settled on the bed, legs crisscrossed. "Shiny," she says, looking at the diamond pendant Andrew gave me before leaving for Japan two weeks ago. "It reminds me of the ring Paul bought you in Thailand." Manu looks around the room, assessing all the objects. Mum's gathered my traveling notebooks and photo albums in a pile. "You want to come and stay at our place tomorrow night?"

Manu and Fred have lived together for so long, they're like a married couple. She can't stay today—she signed up for a pottery workshop before knowing when I'd arrive. I don't remember the last time I did something creative. We make plans for tomorrow. I walk her outside with my pack of cigarettes.

"You're still smoking?"

"I stopped but..." I really did for a week. "It's my last one." I show her the empty pack. I bought it after arguing with Andrew one night. Still, I felt bad for breaking my deal with myself.

"Quit that shit, Lili! Seriously!" She squints and frowns in disgust.

"Last one. After that, I'm done. Seriously."

She points her car keys at me. "I'm picking you up tomorrow morning at 8. We're going for a run!"

I wait for her to leave before lighting my last cigarette. It doesn't taste so good anymore.

Mum opens the door. "No smoking here."

"Mum!"

"No smoking!" She gives me a fierce stare and closes the door.

St Kitts will be a much-needed vacation after ten days here. I don't know why I resisted Andrew on that one. My ticket is non-refundable–I'm definitely going.

Mum and I go shopping later in the afternoon. We enter a home-décor boutique and look at beautiful lace curtains that would fit well in Manu and Fred's new apartment. Mum chooses this moment to ask me the exact questions I have no answer for.

"No, I still don't know what I'll do after modeling.

Yes, things are fine between Andrew and me.

No, I'm not being aggressive. I'm just stressed when I'm asked to think about my future."

I wish we were decorating my own apartment.

Over dinner, Dad starts a conversation about the crash and the crisis that's reached Europe. He took a long nap while Mum and I went shopping and now he has energy to burn. He's opened a lovely bottle of Chinon and I am careful not to drink too much–I still remember my pathetic drunken scene on the rooftop, the night Andrew closed the deal with Japan. I alternate each of my two glasses with a large glass of water. Mum's made the best Boeuf Bourguignon she's ever made.

"Americans will bounce back," I tell Dad. "In France, it's different. They wait to see what the country can do for them."

My parents are used to me criticizing the French attitude. This is how most of our political conversations end up. Can we not talk about something else?

After dinner, we watch a French movie with a very French ending: she dies, he lives, everyone's miserable. Perhaps there's a sliver of hope–Mum sees one–but it's not obvious.

In bed, I try to Skype with Andrew, but it's the wrong time for him. I pick up one of the photo albums in the middle of the pile on the shelves, entitled "Australia".

I had never seen a sky so vast as Australia's pale blue infinity. I had never been called *guys* or *folks* before and I had never heard an accent with the resonance of holidays. It sounded breezy, joyous and confident. I wanted the specters of the Vietnam War and Cambodian Genocide to rest behind me, along with the ghosts of my arguments with Paul, too many and too painful. We were to start fresh on our fourth month of traveling–tabula rasa.

The world of the Great Barrier Reef, entirely made of living organisms, opened up from the Tropic of Capricorn to the South of Papua New Guinea and spread over two hundred kilometers. Depending on the algae or other hosts that attached to the billions of little coral animals, their shades ranged from blue to purple, yellow, and translucent green–it was a live fireworks show in the ocean.

I was cautious at first: it was my first time snorkeling. I didn't know how to dive and jumped in the water with the grace of a seal. Everything became easier when I saw the first fish. It was as if I were entering a most sacred place. A long fish with a leopard-like spots passed by me, very close. I could almost touch it. Or rather, it almost touched me. Leopard fish, Rainbow fish and Butterfly fish– every one of them was a wonder. Even the sound of the ocean was new to me. My breathing muffled and waffled in the water. All the living colors of the ocean, all the shapes and sizes that had so far been foreign to me filled me with a burst of happiness. The grace of the inhabitants of the reef attracted me, like the Enneads had attracted Ulysses' men. I wanted to follow them, be them, be with them forever, but Paul caught my attention waving at me frantically under water. We went to the surface. He said I was going too far. He repeated what the instructor on the boat had told us about the perimeter. I swam back, closer to the boat and then once again forgot about humankind as I resumed my snorkeling. I was in a merry-go-round that sped up and slowed down in one same ride, in a festival of colors where Fire fish, Painted rays, and Blue stars were kings, playing in harmony with seaweeds and bright corals. I was touching heaven underwater, a place impermeable to time.

Paul was growing more and more distant with me. I was trying to understand the elastic effect and the concept of the cave—some phenomenon from a self-help book I had found on a shelf at a backpacker's place—but I could not talk to Paul about it, and lost interest in the book. I also didn't know then what it meant to be co-dependent. All I knew was that I didn't want to wait outside a cave for Paul to come out and pay attention to me again. I wasn't patient with him; I'd call, and even scream, for him to come close to me again, so I could stop feeling as lonely and isolated as I felt then.

When we came back to the shore, I was attracted by a fashion photo-shoot that a small crowd had gathered around. I approached slowly to see the model. She was moving as if we weren't there. How could she move around in her bathing suit and ignore all the people staring at her? She was incredibly sexy: her lips were slightly parted, her eyes coolly appraising the camera. Confidence oozed out of her as she turned this way and that. It was like watching art in motion. Watching her put me in a trance. I wanted to be her, to be like her, to have her confidence and sex appeal.

Paul and I had purchased a van to travel through Australia. It was expensive, but it seemed like the most cost-efficient option at the time, while offering the freedom we were each looking for. Australia was more expensive than we had expected—I needed to budget our lifestyle, month by month now. With this new expense, I feared we would run out of money before we reached New Zealand, which meant that we would have to work for a while at some point during our time in Australia. I scribbled down a few ideas of jobs that I could do for a short period of time, such as fruit-picking, but Paul didn't think I could physically handle it. Maybe I could teach in private schools, work in a bookstore, lead visits in a museum, or read to children in libraries, although I wasn't sure one got paid for that. I kept thinking of the girl I had seen on the beach. I wanted to add modeling to my list, but it didn't seem realistic.

Paul was sitting there, in his chair, content. He had his routine: coffee and a book in the morning, beer and the papers in the afternoon. He wasn't worried one bit. "Trust me. I've done this before and that's what everyone else does: you buy a van and you sell it. You may lose some money, but you may gain some too." I wasn't aware that we were gambling. "We'll have enough for New-Zealand. I don't see what's your problem."

"My problem, as you say, is that we don't know for sure if we'll be able to sell it or not."

"We can die tomorrow. Ok?"

And I was the one being so French and dramatic?

Paul didn't know that when I was younger, my parents used to own an apartment in the mountain. This was where we would spend every Christmas, the four of us. Those were the best Christmases. We had our ritual: ski up and down the pistes every day, from morning to dusk, decorate the tree, wait for Mum in the corridor on Christmas Eve while she pretended she had forgotten something inside, when in fact she was putting the presents under the tree, go out for cheese fondue and cheap chocolate treats in colorful foil paper and come back to the apartment to find magic under the tree. It was my favorite holiday. There was no TV, no homework, just us, talking and playing games every night. Dad was relaxed, Mum barely had any cooking to do and Manu and I slept on bunk beds, not in two separate rooms.

Dad used to tell Mum that she worried too much about money, especially the lack of it. He would say things like, "We're fine. Trust me." But one day, they had to sell the apartment. I thought we were becoming poor and worried that we'd then have to leave our house. We had always had enough until one day, out of the blue, as far as I could tell, we no longer did. How could I know if Paul and I would be ok tomorrow?

I imagined the amazing life the girl modeling on the beach must have had. I could hear my friend Milly in London talk about her positive words theory and the word *realistic* sounded terrible to me. What if I erased it from my dictionary and dreamt a little more?

Paul got up and came back with two more beers. He held one out for me. I inhaled the smell of the foam on the top and in the same breath wrote down "modeling". I didn't tell Paul. Not until we reached New Zealand.

I wish I could tell my younger self to relax. I was so scared to take the leap. But I did it, I followed that inner voice, that guttural feeling that would not quit me, and I guess it worked out pretty ok. In a strange way, I miss her a little. She was braver than I feel now–I don't want to relive the same heartaches, and I don't want to feel the pain of loneliness.

A photo of me dancing and smiling with children around a bonfire slips off the album–a photo Paul sent me after his return to London. I really don't laugh much with Andrew: no more weekend-getaways in the woods or to the beach, no more running by the river together, no more lazy morning in bed. Everything is about work, every conversation.

I turn off the light, but I can't sleep. I'm jet-lagged. The diamond around my neck doesn't feel right. I unclip the chain and put the necklace on the nightstand. I turn the light back on and reopen the photo-album on Australia.

A few clouds had stroked the somber sky. It was going to be a beautiful sunrise. A team of men was inflating three hot air balloons on a vast, dry plain. They had to hurry– the sky was lightening fast. It was so quiet, I felt we had surprised nature during her toilette while she dusted herself with pastel hues that glowed as the sky brightened.

The balloons grew like giant peaches and passengers clambered in. One flew up then another and then it was our turn to hop in the gondola. Paul had packed his cameras in his backpack and got in easily with his long legs. He would ask if I was ok, but never offer a hand. I didn't know where all his gentle manners had gone. I was getting much fitter anyway. The basket, deep and heavy, lifted off awkwardly and I leaned over the edge, watching the ground recede. Trees and people got smaller, perspectives changed and the sky grew bigger. We were flying with windows open wide onto the world. The burner above our head was the engine of the vehicle. Every few minutes, with a roar, it turned the air boiling hot. Across the dirigible ran a 'no smoking' sign on a metal bar—as if anyone would have. The pilot pulled and released a handle in the manner of a train conductor to navigate. The hot air released into the mouth of the balloon generated buoyancy—this allowed us to float, he explained. My cheeks and eyes would burn each time I got too close to the middle. The intense red vermillion at the top of the balloon would fade against the blue edges of the raising flames and fire bolts would disappear against the wall, so thin and yet so resistant. I leant over the basket to cool off and felt the adrenaline from the novelty rush through me. Mornings were my favorite time of the day. Anything was possible in the morning.

The sky was shedding fast its deep pink and purple shades for vibrant oranges. Paul placed an arm over my shoulders and pointed at a small brown spot. Two kangaroos were hopping in fields of mangoes and bananas. From up here, they looked like rabbits. Another balloon, red vermillion, floated by us, and it was seconds before Paul picked up his camera.

I did not want to think about my eventual return to France, but I had to. Mum had sent me a new email to remind me that I had six months to make a decision. The teaching school in France was waiting for my answer. I still didn't have any. I knew I had much better chances of passing the exam if I went to the preparatory school for a year. Dad was recovering pretty well, she wrote in another paragraph. He was back to work. She longed to see me and I felt a tightening in my chest, as if I had come back to the surface too fast. I was hoping for something to happen to help me reach a decision and that somehow I would "know".

The thought of returning to Europe felt like going back to an ex-boyfriend. There were so many things I missed and loved there, besides my friends and family, but I could not shake off that impression. It felt I would not thrive there and I wanted to keep exploring, but what other options did I have? Without an alternative, there was no choice to make. I couldn't simply decide not to teach.

I don't want to change my life all over again, but I must find out what makes me happy. I am more independent now, but what good is freedom without a purpose and an intention?

Another blast of burning air screamed through the balloon. I looked up. In the bright blue sky, someone, or something, higher than us was pulling the strings, altering shapes and setting colors on fire, laying splashes of red along the horizon. The energy I felt did not just live up there in the sky but also down in the oceans and rivers and in the woods and atop mountains. It felt so powerful.

Chapter 18

little sugar, good quality dark chocolate, eggs at room temperature and dark liquor–Mum uses Grand Marnier–is all we need for a chocolate mousse. Manu came early this morning to help in the kitchen. We have a few hours ahead of us before the guests arrive. Manu whips the egg whites and I'm melting the cacao au bain-marie. We both know the best part is yet to come. Mum slowly incorporates the whites to the yolks in the chocolate bowl. My sister and I look at the bowl like two rascals. Who will be first to dip her fingers in it? "You're not licking that," Mum warns. "How old are you, girls?" I say seven and skip the twenty before. Manu says two, forgetting three decades. Mum pours the mix in a deep glass bowl. Game on! I'm courteous and let her have the wooden spoon. My fingers are first in the bowl though. The phone rings. We look at each other and wait. Mum gives up and goes to pick it up.

The bowl is sparkling when she comes back, holding out the phone for me. "It's Andrew." I take the phone to my room.

I come back to the kitchen a few minutes later and wish there were some chocolate left to lick. Mum and Manu look at me with question mark on their forehead. "His plans changed. He actually came back yesterday and he's spending Christmas with his cousins in Connecticut."

Mum passes her soft hand on my cheek like she used to do when I was sad. Her morning smell, imbued with her familiar perfume, relaxes me.

The front door opens. Dad's back from the boulangerie. He opens the white paper bag underneath my nose—the scent of warm buttery croissants and pains au chocolat makes everything a little better, for now.

"Merry Christmas!" I say as I open the front door at 12.30 sharp. Pépé, Grandma, Aunt Brigitte, her husband and my cousin have arrived. I'd rather hug than kiss to feel them closer to my heart, but it's not the custom here.

"It looks like it's going to rain," Grandma says. It was sunny just a few hours ago; the weather can change fast here. "You've lost weight," she continues.

Pépé tells her to leave me alone. Mum pats her hands dry on her red and pink apron before greeting everyone. The curls of her short haircut are messy from the steam raging in the kitchen—her territory—and matted on her forehead. She blows some air to her forehead. The hallway smells of red wine reduction and roasted venison. I offer to take scarves and coats to my room.

"Where's Andrew?" Aunt Brigitte asks.

"He had to work," I answer from my bedroom.

I hear them speaking in low voices as they move in to the living room and choose to ignore it when I come back. Manu has left to go pick up Fred from the train station— he was spending Christmas Eve with his family. An Italian rock CD is on, Dad is humming the lyrics he doesn't know, and pops open a Clairette de Die—his preferred alternative to champagne. He's already opened a bottle of apple cider and served his father. The tree I decorated with Mum illuminates the room in silver and blue lights. I tell Pépé about the over-sweetened cider I tasted with Sarah in a farm near the Hudson River and he says that if the farmer came over to his house, he'd show him how to make the real thing. Baubles and garlands twinkle intermittently like little lights of caution reminding me to enjoy this moment with my family.

"Where have you been lately?" Uncle Thomas asks.

I sit down next to him on the edge of the couch while Dad serves bubbly wine to everyone, except my little cousin who's only allowed fruit juice. "Let's see..." I really have to make a mental inventory.

"It's hard to keep up with you," my aunt says. "You're always away or back from somewhere else."

"As if you lived in parallel universes," my little cousin adds. He must have been watching lots of TV.

"When I call your mother sometimes she doesn't always know where you are," Aunt Brigitte continues. "You are on a perpetual round-the-world-trip."

Mum, who is just coming out of the kitchen, confesses that it's hard to keep up with me. She sets up a few bowls on the table: cheese crackers, olives, small Frankfurt sausages, tomatoes and mozzarella on toothpicks and warm petit fours.

"Only my booker can keep track." Mum forgot the *saucisson.* I get up. "He knows my schedule better than me even." On paper, living between France and New York sounds glamorous, but the reality of living in-between two places is that my heart is split between each side of the Atlantic. I can't help but wish for Andrew to be here.

"Do you have any time to spend at home?" Grandma asks when I come back from the kitchen with the small plate of charcuterie.

I sit down next to her. "Barely!"

"It must be hard for relationships," she says.

There's a knock on the windowpane. Manu's come back with Fred and their hands are full of presents. I leap off the couch to meet them and as soon as they close the door the rain begins to fall.

"Expect heavy showers all week," the radio had warned. It had been raining for days. Everything in the van was damp: the bed sheets, my clothes and Coco Pops. Queensland was flooding and Paul and I arguing, suffering from what he called "cabin fever."

"You are so insensitive!" I would say.

"You're smothering me," he'd reply. "I need space!"

"It's Australia—how much space do you need?"

The windshield wipers were flapping like angry bats. Paul kept his jaw tight, his eyes fixed on the road and both his hands on the wheel. He maneuvered around the crevasses in the road fairly well at first, but when we drove through an intersection so flooded it resembled a creek, water started coming up through the floor of the van and the engine coughed. The windscreen was a fog. I begged Paul to slow down but he wouldn't listen to me. I opened my window and water came splashing in. The van was coughing. I rolled up the window and we were suffocating again inside. The van made a weird gargling sound and the wheels slipped off the tarmac. It sounded like the van was vomiting the engine. And then, we came to a stop.

We could not restart the van; we had to be rescued by a ranger.

I fly out to St. Kitts in two days; I should be excited but I'm not. There is all that space between Andrew and me—too much of it. What is going to rescue us? Is it braver to leave or stay in this relationship and work out our differences? My visit home has gone by so quickly. Today especially, with all my family around on Christmas Day, went really fast.

I've disconnected from the rest of the world and now feel the need to check my online account. I have a new friend request. The clock in my chest goes berserk when I see the name. It's been five years since I last saw Paul. I stare at this profile picture and turn off my phone. Do I want to be his "friend"?

The phone—the house-phone—rings. I look at the time on my ancient alarm clock on the bedside table. It's close to midnight: at least two hours too late to receive a phone call. In my parents' bedroom upstairs, the wooden floor creaks softly—Mum's up. Only Andrew could be calling at this time, if he's forgotten about the time difference. My cell phone is off so it could be him except that we already spoke today and we rarely talk more than once a day. I wait to see if Mum will be coming down the stairs. Instead, heavier footsteps sound on the floor. Both Mum and Dad are up now. I push the sheets and blanket off and wrapping a robe around me, go to see what's happening.

Chapter 19

It's a cold and windy day at the beach. I wrap my scarf around my neck, button my jacket all the way up, pull on my gloves and tighten my grip around Dad's arm. He took the week off. I called Steven to say I would fly straight from Paris to Cape Town for my next job, instead of going back to New York. Then I called Andrew to say I wouldn't meet him in St Kitts. He said that he was sorry and that he'd work as hard as he could while I was away so we could spend some time together when I got back.

We buried Pépé yesterday.

He passed away in his sleep and I guess there is some comfort in that and the fact that we spent Christmas all together.

Dad and I turn around at the American flag on the beachfront—one of the many that commemorate D-Day. The wind now pushes us along the jetty. "Andrew told me to give you his condolences."

"Is he doing ok?"

I nod yes. Pépé's last few words resound. *Does he treat you right?* He does his best. I touch my throat underneath my scarf and realize I haven't worn his necklace since I took it off the first night I came to Normandy.

"I'm sorry you cancelled your vacation."

"There'll be plenty more opportunities," I say. "Right now, I just want to be here with you." I look at the ground so Dad doesn't see my emotions. I notice a stem of Poinsettia flower at my feet and pick it up as years of repressed guilt and worry surface. "I'm sorry I wasn't there when you were at hospital. I should have come back."

"I never expected you to."

"I know you didn't want me there." I feel the pointy edge of the star-shaped leaves.

Dad stops. His eyes have sunk so deep they shine brighter. He turns to me. "I didn't want you there because I didn't want you to cut your trip short for me. Nothing else." The wind blows a few strands of my hair across my face. "Coline, you know how much I love you, right?" A contraction in my gut makes me crunch up. "Munchkin…" I always want him to be proud of me. I don't think he knows that. He pulls me into a big hug. "I knew that if I asked you to come back, you would. That was enough for me." I detach gently from his hug. We don't usually show so much display of affection–Dad wasn't brought up that way.

"I'm sorry. I'm a crying machine." We let out a little laugh, a little gasp for air.

"I am so proud of you."

"Dad, you don't know…"

"Coline, I don't need to know anything other than what I already know about you. You're much stronger than you think you are and you don't give yourself enough credit. I also know that you'll figure it out with Andrew. Like you did with Paul." The tide is high and the clouds are low. We resume our promenade in the brisk air of Luc-Sur-Mer.

Five years ago, at that same time, I was with Paul in Vietnam. We had spent Christmas on a boat in Halong Bay. I was sick and cold. By the fake tree inside the boat, I promised myself never to spend another Christmas away from home. Last year, I compromised. This year, Andrew didn't. Our talks about starting a family together lie very far behind. He'll be tanning in the Caribbean sun for New Year's Eve and I'll be with the people I care most about and who show, unconditionally and repeatedly, their love for me.

Dad points at the Christmas flower I am still holding. Memories of the ceremony I witnessed with Paul weave through my consciousness. I tell Dad about the flower and incense offerings the Thais placed on the river to express gratitude and the prayers they chanted all night long.

"If we had a little candle, we could do that," I say. It probably sounds silly to Dad. No one talks about "God" or uses the word "pray" in my family. If Pépé was buried, it is only because it is a tradition.

"With Brigitte, we said a little prayer for Dad after the ceremony, just between us." He reaches for something in the inside pocket of his coat. "I don't know why, but I kept this." He holds out a half-consumed tea-light candle—those that the church provides for memorial services. I could not believe he had taken it with him.

The English Channel rises before us. I take a lighter I had left in my pocket and together we walk down the few stairs carved out of the stone wall to the beach. The sand is hard underneath our feet. We crouch and light the candle, set it on the red flower, and let it sail away. I pray that it meets Pépé's spirit. Dad closes his eyes and bright shiny tears course down his cheeks. I take his hand and together we stand and walk away.

We both need some sweetness. Dad buys me a *gui-gui*, the famous hard marshmallow of Luc-Sur-Mer, a candy twisted with flavored colors around a stick. This tastes much better than a cigarette. We slowly drive back home to Mum and Manu, our temple of love.

Chapter 20

I'm leaving France in the rain, my carry-on heavier than when I left New York. I took my traveling notebooks with me, along with a French volume Mum gave me to read. There was no bookmark inside so I took a photo from my trip with Paul—some artwork with a multitude of sign posts oriented in different directions. I decided to accept his friend request.

The flight to Cape Town is a direct one and a chauffeur is picking me up from the airport to the villa. When you're rested and all is taken care of, it's easier to acclimate to new surroundings. I'm shooting for a French catalogue, and the whole team is French, except for the photographer. It'll be hard not to smoke with them, but I've already stopped for two weeks now. Dad gave me a pack of Kiss Cool mints when he dropped me at the airport an hour ago. I miss him already. The rain sounds sad, but the growing crowd at the gate soon muffles it.

Americans might be loud but so are the French. There's a child who just can't keep quiet or sit still and a woman who can't stop texting and a couple who should stop arguing. They're discussing whose fault it is that they had to rush to the gate, when they're both here now, waiting for the plane to arrive. What a waste of time and energy. If we added all the time spent arguing over nothing, I wonder how many years of life and love we would get back. I wonder what Pépé would do differently about his life, if he could—if he even wanted to.

When death enters our life there's a distance between us and everyone else who is not concerned.

The feeling doesn't last, and it's a good thing, but when it's there, time slows down and intensifies every new experience. There's no more that rush to get somewhere. We just *are* and feel more present and alive.

Pépé appears vividly in my memories. The back of his neck is wrinkled like a tree trunk. When I was a little girl sitting in the back of my grand-parents car with Manu, that was all I could see between his seat and the head rest—his wrinkled neck. I wondered if my neck would look like his one day. I didn't work hard in the fields like Pépé. I wish I had written down the stories he told me about the war and that I've forgotten now. I'd have liked to confess to him about the extra sweets I used to steal from the ceramic soup tureen after lunch. "Only one, Coline," he would say. "I counted them. I'll know if you took more than one." Ah, Pépé! Did you really know? I think he's winking at me right now. Perhaps he even told Dad to get me those mints. I can sense him next to me. There must be other ways to communicate than through the use of language.

My phone chimes. Paul wants to live chat with me. He looked at some of my photos. He says I look happy. I've resisted the urge to check his online profile. I write and then erase a few answers before simply asking him how he is. He's not married, but has a little boy. He's still taking pictures. He stopped working at the store and photo lab to freelance for travel magazines.

"I miss backpacking," I write.

"I miss you." Three words that detonate when dropped at random. "I'm sorry it ended that way." That makes two of us. "Do you ever come to London? I'd love to see you again."

My head's spinning between memories of us on the floor, mapping our trip, hiking in Chang Mai and Sapa, the endless arguments we had in Australia, the time we wasted... Am I at the end of my relationship with Andrew? I feel like a mosquito caught in a net. I love him, but I'm not sure that it's enough. The words of one of Jason Mraz's songs play in my head: *It takes no time to fall in love/ But it takes you years to know what love is.* I'm not sure I even know how to love myself.

I check Paul's page. His status says he's in a relationship with Christy Maverick! All this time he was lying. While I take the news in, the screen on my phone goes dark.

My temporary turmoil dissipates in the surrounding agitation—I missed the boarding announcement. A relief comes over me. I'm going on a trip, I have work, a family who loves me—everything is as it should be. I go back on our chat page and answer that I don't ever get to London and that I'm happy for him. I hesitate and add one "X" at the end of my message, which means a cross in my mind, not a kiss.

It's only when I'm on the plane and remove my coat and scarf that I realize I've left the necklace that Andrew gave me on the dressing table in my childhood bedroom.

I lean my forehead against the window. The clouds are too thick to see anything. There are plenty of movie options in the plane, but I'd rather do something creative. I pick up the notebook Mum sent me in New York, but stare at the blank page, both too sad and self-conscious to write or draw anything. I fan through the notebook I filled in Australia.

Paul had taught me a new word and I used it to describe everything we saw in the outback. "How *quaint* was Malanda!" I said, beaming. He smiled. "A town from out-of-time. So *quaint*." We had been following the same route since we had left the coast to avoid another storm, and everything felt new again. The sun was kissing my face through the window frame and Paul's smile felt like sunlight flying straight to my heart.

"Kangaroo!" Paul pointed at a red bush on his right.

"Where?"

"You missed it."

"And the bakery!" Across the street from the hotel marked up by the guidebook was a place with pastries as appetizing as any French bakery. I drooled over their shiny apple turnovers and thick slices of custard pie. I bought one of each for us to share but ended up eating most of them.

"You have such a sweet tooth, sweetheart."

"All my teeth are sweet!" I could still taste the white heavenly dust I slowly licked off my fingers. "The town should enter a patisserie competition, not a 'Who's got the largest wooden structure in the whole southern hemisphere' competition." I even made a note to write to our travel guide for culinary updates.

The hot wind was stroking my hair. The path in front of us was infinite. I could barely believe that we were driving in the Australian desert, the *bush*. It felt pure and freeing. Paul liked to select music from the mini-disc player he plugged into the lighter socket. We rolled our heads and shimmied in our car seats to classics from the Steve Miller Band and

The Stones. I could spend entire hours staring at the road, sometimes with empty thoughts but clear feelings. Other times I'd wonder if I'd ever feel as free as I did then.

I wrote a poem on the next page.

The blowing wind is hot.
The bird, a lorikeet, falters.
The clouds hug and encircle the mountains in their heavy fall.
The trees look so small.
They hold on tight between mother and sisters. The wind is cunning.
The bird… I think he's
falling. But, there, he finds shelter in a tree.
While I wait for him, who may never come back.

We could drive for two hundred kilometers in the desert and never see a soul. The farms we drove past were thousands of times bigger than what we were used to in Europe. We saw road trains in the desert—trucks about five or six wagons long, so big that when they overtook us the van shook. The travel guide said the desert road was very boring, but not to me. I thought the isolated white letterboxes on the side of the road quaint beyond any expectation.

It was easy to disconnect from the rest of the world on the road. We would infrequently go on the Internet, only to realize that nothing much had changed. The same tragedies unfolded on the rest of the planet: suicide bombings in Iraq, train explosions in Iran, Kerry campaigning for President in the US. And singular horror stories: a cannibal had found a man on the Internet, killed him and cooked him with garlic, and a French singer had beaten his girlfriend to death. There was very little good news. Someone should report those stories. I told Paul about my idea to become the editor of the Happy Herald and he thought it was a good one.

We were still four hundred kilometers away from Mount Isa, a melting pot pioneer town of fifty-two nationalities. From Mount Isa, we'd start the long drive back to the coast, heading southeast. In Cloncurry I wanted to visit the Royal Flying Doctor Service, an aeromedical health care center for people living in places so remote, they had no access to medical support. People in this part of the country lived thousands of miles apart from each other, yet they had found ways to stay connected and rescue each other.

When Paul and I went to the supermarket to get food for dinner one night, I found some paint and brushes in the kind of pack you buy for children. I sat down at the table in the van with my paint and notebook, and a glass of water for my brushes. I had no technique, and didn't know what to make, but I knew what colors I wanted to play with, so I started with working on my palette. Nature was one constant source of inspiration throughout my journey. I put on some music in the van and surrendered to the experience.

We were getting more and more familiar with the Aborigines paintings and I wanted to have a go at their "pointillism" technique. I was a kid in the art classroom. I was a kid at the kitchen table while Mum was making dinner. I was a kid with no worries in the world, deeply immersed in my activity. I still remember the peace I felt when I had finished.

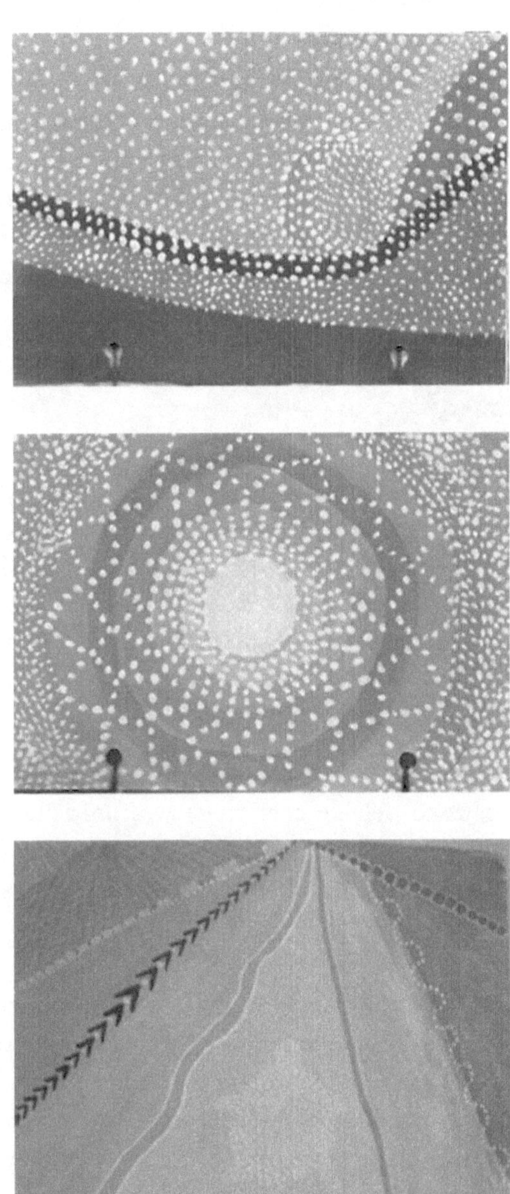

With yet another sense of space and time, Aborigines too formed a community of their own. What is my community? I have a family and will always be a part of it, but I need more than that. At different times, I have considered myself a teacher, a French girl, a backpacker, a model and many other identities of that kind and often found each too limiting. Perhaps I have yet to find the place where I belong and perhaps we can belong to several communities.

I didn't want to believe that there was only one straight path for me—it seemed too grey and too small to live like that. I dreamt of rounder shapes and brighter colors and on paper, it was all possible.

Sometimes, you can be seats away from someone or sharing the same bed and feel completely disconnected. Sometimes, you can speak the same language and not understand each other. I'm not sure Andrew and I have the same ideals. When I started modeling, I became so focused on having financial safety, I forgot to fill up my creative bank account¬¬—a huge contribution to my happiness. I don't want to chase money as if it were an end in itself, and I fear that this is what Andrew is doing.

The smell of boerewors and grilling steaks wafts into my room. Berto, the Brazilian photographer, is helping the production guy with the barbecue, or braai as they call it here. The client rented a beautiful villa in South Africa for us to stay in for the week–a much nicer alternative to a hotel stay. Today was fun: we blew balloons in the desert for the photo shoot and checked in for a helium therapy session afterwards. Our squeaky cartoon voice rubbed against the strings in the wind, while the bright colored balloons danced in the pastel sky.

I started an online video session with Andrew and the conversation moved once more to our cultural differences. "If we had kids together," I say, "I'd want them to have both our cultures."

"Leen, they'll be born here. They'll be Americans," he replies.

"But France is a huge part of my identity."

"They'll be Americans who speak French. You'll teach them."

"You said you would learn some." I feel like a disk on repeat.

"I just wanted you to stop harassing me." Is this what I'm doing? Why do I care so much? This is not about learning French, I realize. "Babe," he resumes in a sweeter tone, "you just lost your grandpa and have been waking up at the crack of dawn every morning this past week. Let's talk about this another time." It's not about language or culture–it's about connection and compassion.

We hang up. I walk down to salsa music in the kitchen, where the stylist and the make up artist are making a salad.

A bottle of Pinotage is already open on the counter top, and I help myself to a glass. They insist on making a toast. We raise our glasses to love, health and freedom.

The sun sets over Cape Town. Every night the sky amazes us with a new show that makes us forget the long day of work we just had. Berto turns up the volume when Tribalistas comes on the playlist and invites us to dance to music from his homeland. He takes my hand. I resist at first—I'm a terrible dancer. "Just follow me." He puts his hand on the small of my back and pulls me in so close to his body I feel uncomfortable and aroused at the same time. "Relax. Just enjoy the music." I breathe deep to quiet my mind and follow Berto's rhythm. "You got it," he says. Dancing is liberating.

The heat subsides and the rest of the crew goes to bed. Berto and I lie on long chairs in front of the pool, wrapped in blankets. A bottle and two glasses sit on a side table. Tomorrow is the last day and we don't have much to shoot. We can sleep in a little. Berto tried earlier to convince me to follow him into the pool—danger zone—but I declined. Staying up with him so late, sharing wine and confidences like two lovers is plenty. If Andrew saw us it would hurt him, I don't want that. Crap! I forgot to ask Mum to send me my necklace. Oh well, that can wait. Roberto closes his eyes, escapes to his own world and I too close my eyes. I imagine how rich my life could be with more peace and more fun. I'm not ready to go back to New York.

The driver is coming shortly to take me to the airport. Shooting with French people—Berto spoke a very decent French—has been much nicer than expected. I felt funny again—funny in a good way. I have missed people laughing at my jokes in French and all the *taquineries, chipoteries* and *conneries* (the teasing, quibbling and stupidities) that come along with our humor. Many French seek other French when they come to New York to recreate a community and speak their own language, but I never did–I wanted to be integrated.

"Do you think life is a result of a multitude of choices we've made that took us where we are right now," Roberto asked last night after we watched a movie, "or is it fate like for Allie and Noah?" I wanted to laugh. Andrew would never say such a thing.

"If things are meant to be," I said, "something higher governs us. If they happen because we make them happen, there's no God."

I balance the two options. I don't think I need an answer. Either we are more powerful than we know or something else is: both views hold infinite possibilities.

An engine roars. Ben, the driver who ferried us around all week, has arrived. I say my goodbyes to the team. The ocean rolls and billows ahead and below, and the mountain on my left encircles the bay. Clouds have a playful way of hovering above Table Mountain, so long and low they cover it like a cloth. The scene reminds me of a poem I wrote in Australia.

In a sky so blue, so large,
A purple sea surfaces
Underlining the emerging mountains.
Scattered cloud flakes drift
Above a far off mapped out horizon.
A deep serenity seeps into this soft unspoken page,
While a wild vegetation stands strong and protective.

At the beat of nature, the curtain rises and closes—
Its heart, an everlasting well of offerings.

I sit up front next to Ben. There are deep furrows in his forehead and at the side of his mouth. Happy, percussion-heavy music plays from the car stereo. I feel sad to leave. "It's such a beautiful country," I say.

"Oh yes, but you know, it's not easy to live here." Ben turns down the volume. "What you saw is only the shiny side of the coin. Most of the people in Cape Town are poor." He opens a bag of roasted peanuts and offers me some. "Did you go see the townships?"

I thank him and take a small handful. "I heard it's not very safe."

"They're sort of mini-cities made of shacks. They were meant for non-white people during Apartheid. The Cape Flats are where you find them."

"Where do you live, Ben?"

"I live quite far away from the city, up in the mountains over there. I cannot afford to live down here. The government has allowed foreigners to buy properties so prices keep rising and now we can afford even less than we could before."

"When did Apartheid stop?" I feel stupid for asking but it's better than not knowing.

"Oh, about fifteen years ago. It started during WWII. The Dutch Afrikaans wanted to *separate*—that's what *apartheid* means in Afrikaans—from the colored folks."

"I was reading a bit about your history, and how several nationalities came here. And how the integration between the groups was complicated—the black people, the Bushman, the Asian, the Dutch, the French, the English…"

"Oh, yes. But at the same time it's really simple. It all started with the white man. He came and took the Bushman's land–we call them the San now. Then, the black man came. Now, no one understands each other. They all have the right to be here. The blacks are very angry, which you can understand, but it's not making them move forward…"

Ben takes a sip of water from his bottle. "But there are great things happening here," he says, "like art!" He turns up the volume and starts bobbing his head and tapping his hands against the wheel to the beat of the drums. "People have so much experience to express and talent in music, dancing, painting. It's world-class, I tell you."

While I was traveling through Laos, Vietnam and Cambodia, I was obsessed with the war and terrified of violence, shutting myself off from all the riches those countries had to offer. I will not find the answers I am looking for if I keep being scared of the future. The state of the unknown is just a state of mind–there's no more reason to fear it, than to embrace it.

"This music makes me want to dance," I say.

"You must tell your boyfriend to take you out dancing!" I smile politely. "You're going back to France?"

"No, New York. That's where I live."

"And your boyfriend, what is he? American?" I nod yes. "He speaks French with you?" I shake my head no. "But you must miss your country?"

"Of course." I am a different person when I speak French and that is a part of me Andrew will never know.

At the airport, Ben helps me with my luggage and gives me a strong warm handshake. "Go dancing, Miss!"

I laugh. "I'm not a good dancer."

He smiles. "If we waited to be good at something, we wouldn't do anything!"

Chapter 21

"What are you making?" I was listening to a playlist of old French songs and didn't hear Andrew come home.

"Beef Bourguignon," I announce and lift up the lid. Mum shared her recipe with me. He hovers his face over the pot of red wine reduction, dips a spoon and licks it, humming with pleasure.

"While it simmers, come see—I've got something for you," he says, leading me down the hall.

"Happy Valentine's!" he says, and proudly reveals a plant as large as a small tree. "Do you like it? You told me you missed nature so, *voilà*! I know you said no gifts, but this is different." He pauses. "You don't seem too excited."

"I am. I'm just… surprised." I give him a kiss. "It's perfect. Really. Thank you."

I did not expect such a sweet gesture from him; this realization saddens me when it should give me hope. We go back to the kitchen, open a bottle, light candles on the table and the windowsill and sit down for dinner. The meat is tender and the herbs have perfumed it just right.

"You're wearing your necklace again." He grins awkwardly.

"It got here this morning." I told Andrew Mum had been very busy and didn't have time to go to the post office, when in truth I kept forgetting to ask her to mail it to me.

Andrew's phone vibrates on the table. He checks his message, puts it away and asks "Did you go to your agency?"

"Next week."

"I think it's slow for everyone, you know."

"I don't think Steven's pushing me hard enough. We get in a rut sometimes. I need to shake things up a bit and have Steven take new Polaroids—what?"

He stares at me over his glass of wine. "You're so cute when you're all business. And when you pout, like right now. And when you roll your eyes."

"Do you want more meat?" He says no.

A candle flickers out and Andrew's face darkens. "Coline, is there something I should know?"

He takes my hand over the table and I stroke the back of his with my thumb. Since I came back from South Africa, I couldn't help but be a little distant. I know he's picked up on it. There's nothing to say. "I'm a little stressed about work, that's all," I lie.

We stare intently at each other. He takes me to the bedroom and makes love to me. When he's about to come I fake an orgasm and afterwards we lie in bed, quiet. Does he know?

I thought Andrew might have gone to sleep when he says "I've been promoted." I congratulate him and he explains the extra responsibilities he has been given. All I hear is that he is going to be traveling more and working even later than he already is. I can't blame him for wanting to be more successful—this is what I've been thriving for as well—but we already have a good life, financially speaking. There is no end to wanting more and it doesn't serve any purpose. Money is such a masquerade.

I turn the light off and the sound of the heater fills up the room. It feels I am slowly giving up on us. When I dreamt of teaching, and later of modeling, I had a goal and a purpose in life–I was going to serve in public schools, and explore the world. I have neither today and I don't know which steps to take to feel good about myself again. I travel all over the world and yet, my inner world feels so small and so tight.

The cup warms my hands through the gloves. I blow on the hot chocolate and the steam warms my frozen face. It snowed all day yesterday, enough to transform Madison Square Park into one big marshmallow. Bundled up in my long down jacket, my favorite scarf around my neck and a hat underneath my furry hood, only my face suffers from the cold dry air. I don't want to go home.

Except for a man in a long, patched up grey wool coat and red hat, the park is desolate. A shopping trolley filled with plastic bags is parked beside him. What life did he have before coming here? Would I be out on a bench or in a shelter, if I were him? I smile. Am I not on a bench in the cold right now?

I went to my agency today to have a meeting with Steven, my booker. I haven't had a job since the catalogue shoot in South Africa. It's been a month. I always fear that this could be the beginning of the end. Steven explained to me what I already knew about the holidays being a slow time and fashion week too, since I don't do the runways. I came in with a list of clients that I thought were possible for us to get and suggested we approach them again.

Steven shuffled through my portfolio to see if we should move some pictures around and get rid of some old ones. "What about these clients?" I said, pointing at the top of my list.

He glanced at my list and then stared back at my book. "They think you read too young." He pulled out a headshot of me smiling.

That sounded like rubbish to me, but I had to agree that if this was the truth, it was not necessarily a bad problem to have. I kept going with my list.

"You're a little too old for them, Coco. They loved you as a junior, but now you've got curves... Besides, they're changing art directors, so we should wait."

It was a little hard to hear but these are the rules of the industry. I've learned not to take criticisms too personally, but I don't like it when Steven gives me mixed answers. Last week, another client said I was too skinny. Which one is it? Am I too old, too fat, or both? Or is it the art director who doesn't like me? Sometimes it's a straight answer and other times it's not: the fashion industry is crazy.

Sarah, my model-friend, is working a lot more consistently than me, I noticed. She is with a different agency, but we also look very different. It's impossible to compare.

"So, who's good for me?" I asked Steven, at the end of our meeting.

"You're in between two age groups, honey–it's hard."

What's hard is to know if my agent is still on my team, doing his best for me, or if his focus has shifted to other girls–"new faces," like I once was.

"Don't worry, it'll pick up again. It always does." He was typing at his computer. "I'll resend your book with the new material we got from the test you did last week." He leafed through the new sexier pictures he placed in the book and said, "You look great." I held my breath, unsure. "In the meantime, we have another audition for you on Friday—I'll send you the script Dorian sent me. It's perfect for you—it's a French model."

"I can't act." I thought I had done well at the last audition but I didn't make it to the call back. I wasn't good enough to play my own part of a French model.

"Oh sweetie, just be yourself and with that lovely accent of yours, they'll all fall in love with you!"

"But I don't sound right. It's embarrassing."

He spun in his chair to face me. "So why don't you take some acting classes? You said you'd look into that."

"Because..." I was going to say because I'm not good at it. But now the words of Ben, the driver in Cape Town, resonated. If I wait to be good at something, I'll never do anything. I did not know how to pose when I started, but I learned over time. I fantasized about modeling for years before I finally gave it a try. How many more years am I going to resist what I find exciting today, even though it scares me?

I can't stand the ups and downs of my job. If I worked in another field, I would be building a career. I am not going to get any younger or skinnier.

I'm cold. I should go home.

A cold gust of wind lifts some newspapers off the ground. My hair flies across my face. I take a sip of hot chocolate, a sip of comfort. Never mind the calories—I must be burning plenty just trying to stay warm. I'd like to walk to the man on the bench and share my cup with him, but I'm too shy. What if he felt insulted and told me to bugger off? From the west entrance of the park, two Michelin men approach the man on the bench. One of them carries a dark package under his arm.

"Come with us, Francis," I hear him say. "You'll freeze here, buddy."

Francis crosses his arms. "I'm not going anywhere."

The man unfolds the blanket that was tucked under his arm and wraps it over Francis' shoulders. "It's nice and warm, Francis. Don't you agree?"

The other man bends over him and whispers something to coax him to follow them. They must be packed in the shelters. People who once had a job, a family, for whom one day something went wrong and before they had time to fix it, everything had gone wrong.

The man from the shelter straightens up. "You can leave whenever you want," he says. "Just come and be warm tonight, Francis. Just for one night." Francis, arms clasped around his waist, looks up at the white sky and down at his cart. "We'll help you carry your stuff, don't worry about it, buddy." Francis finally gets up, surrendering. The two men help him carry his plastic bags to their van and leave the empty cart behind. What can I do?

A thick trail of chocolate runs down the bottom of my cup. My face and hands are numb. A cold wind pierces through my down jacket and clears my mind of all its thoughts, leaving but one voice, the one that suggests that maybe I don't love Andrew anymore. I stand up, throw the cup away, and head toward the subway entrance. A sticker with a red apple contouring a white heart—the same one I've seen on Sarah's fridge—catches my attention at the top of the stairs. New York Cares organization is looking for volunteers, it reads.

Chapter 22

I take off my hat, gloves, scarf, jacket, fleece and sweater and fold my bike. The snow that was covering the city two weeks ago has completely melted away in the sunny sky of the last few days. I'm given a locker for my bag and a place to leave my bike. A team leader hands me an apron, a hair net and a pair of plastic gloves. It's just after nine, but when I head downstairs into the huge kitchen, it's already a hive of activity as volunteers peel, chop and cook food. I'm given a knife and a box of apples and oranges and I get to work.

I kept tossing in bed last night. The weekend had started so well but then changed course. Andrew and I were walking, both still buzzing from sex that morning and with no plans for the rest of the day, for once, when Mike called and left a voicemail inviting us to dinner that night.

"Just say we're not in town," I pleaded.

"I can't. He's my boss."

"And I'm your girlfriend." Andrew looked at me as if I had said something crazy. "Weekends are for relaxation and fun, not work."

"Mike's fun to be around." Yes, if his wife is not there. The conversation always revolves around the next deal. "It's just dinner, babe."

What language was I supposed to speak to be understood? "Can we not have one full day just you and me?" Andrew had been to Japan again and when he got back last week he dived right back into work. I've barely seen him. I'm struggling to sustain a connection with him.

"I'm here with you right now. Isn't that enough?"

I had heard that before and I could not take it one more time. "No. It's not enough."

Andrew stared at me with defiance, as if challenging me to go against his will. I held my ground—it was taking all the strength I had. I didn't want to fight, but I could not let him manipulate me as he always did, making me feel that I was either being unsupportive or unreasonable. "Fine," he said. "I can meet him for lunch tomorrow when you're gone doing your thing."

"First time here?" the man across from me asks. "You look flushed."

His name is Tony. I explain that I rode my bike from the Seaport to St John the Divine on 112th Street. St Francis church was closer but they didn't need any more volunteers today. Tony volunteers here every week. I am amazed by his dedication. On the other side of the kitchen, three guys are working the stove and oven. They are cooking eggs, bacon and potatoes. I reach for an apple in the fruit tray in front of me and cut it in cubes. I get lost in the repetition of the task. "Ten minutes until we start service," the team leader announces. We all pick up the pace and Tony begins combining all the diced fruit in an enormous bowl.

We line up the trays of bread, fruit salad, scrambled eggs, bacon, gravy, coffee and juice for breakfast in the big room where a seemingly endless stream of people are lining up.

I've been assigned to serving bread rolls. It's an easy task because there's so much bread, I can give the diners plenty. It's trickier for those who serve eggs, where a little has to go a long way. Some people look pretty down and out; others look like regular professionals. All look hungry. Two people from the clergy welcome everyone and say a short and loving prayer.

When the service is over, I walk outside with my fold up bike. An ambulance drives by, siren blaring, lights flashing. While I take a breath in, someone else's life is ending. I breathe out. A baby is born. I'm supposed to meet Andrew and Mike for coffee in the Meatpacking District. A ray of sun comes out from behind the clouds and warms my face. It'll be spring in a couple of months. I feel the tire on my bike and get the pump out. I'm glad I don't own a car; it's much easier to fix a bike.

We had been in Australia for two months. I lay awake in bed, exhausted but restless. Perhaps one day I'd look back on this episode and laugh or understand why it had to happen, but that night it felt like the adventure was coming to an end and I was miserable. We had been driving for a few hours—the day was hot, we were hot and the van was hot too. Paul finally pulled over when there was smoke coming out from the engine. The van had over-heated so badly we had to get towed to a garage for the night. Paul said he'd use money from his saving account and that I could pay him back later, since I had almost nothing left. It was a temporary solution, but I hated the new dependence it created. I already relied on Paul for so many things; I needed him to keep traveling—I was too scared to be on my own.

In many cultures girls were taken from their father to be given to their husband. They never lived on their own, by their own rules. What had I done so far? I had lived with my parents, been the little sister over-protected by her mother, left to London for a year, met Paul within a few months and gone away with him. I wasn't strong like Christy, or many of the other women we met in our travels who seemed so brave, so undaunted. I did not trust that I could travel by myself. I was the one who followed.

The mechanic knocked on the door of the van early the next morning. "It's the engine, folks. I don't have a second-hand one I can sell you. Bit of a bugger really. I can get you a new one, but it'll cost you."

"How much?" Paul asked.

"You'd be looking at least at two grand, maybe more." That was around 10,000 francs—a third of what I had initially saved to go traveling.

We walked away from the gas pumps to have a cigarette. Paul puffed furiously. He didn't try to bargain with the mechanic. He was in shock. I felt as if the earth was opening underneath my feet.

Paul did not want to do odd jobs. We looked in the papers for more serious offers, but they all required a working visa that we didn't have. When the mechanic returned with the van a week later, the bill was higher than he had quoted. I now owed Paul so much money I felt sick just thinking about it. I had made a budget and I had lost all my money. How had this happened?

During the weeks that followed, I could not quiet the voice that was urging me to take a chance at modeling. When I was ten, a photographer approached me while I was on vacation with my family, and encouraged me to model. My parents were polite but firm¬—they had higher hopes for me, hopes that did not include modeling. A similar encounter happened again at fourteen, and again, I had to ignore the voice my own desire, my curiosity to pursue this dream, because my parents wouldn't let me. Now this dream was turning into an obsession: I had to give it a try, at least once in my life. If it did not work out, I would stop wondering about it, but if it did, it could solve so many worries: I would have money to pay off my debts, a job alternative to teaching, and I could keep traveling. And maybe, just maybe, things would get better with Paul.

We sold the van in Sydney for half of what we bought it for, not even covering the cost of the new engine. Apparently, it wasn't a great time to sell. We flew to New Zealand broke, but at least we both had work visas. We'd have to start looking for work once we landed in Auckland: we couldn't afford not to. On our first morning in Auckland, we walked to the docks. Paul stared at the yachts and I at the ferries that would soon leave to Waiheke and Rangitoto islands. The light was playing between the masts and mizzens. Paul pulled out his digital camera from his backpack and adjusted his settings to shoot the bay. To my surprise, he called me next to him and turned the camera on us. The light was good, he said. We looked at the picture in the screen, but I couldn't see what made us a couple. Neither of us looked happy.

I told him about my desire to give modeling a chance.

"Sweetheart, just call your parents," he said. I did and asked for less than what I needed, out of shame. I felt somewhat relieved when I hung up the phone, but soon, I'd run out of money again. And then a thought came to me: if by playing safe I had lost all my money, what did I have to lose by taking a big chance?

We were hungry and walked back up Queen Street to the town center. We stopped at a Dunkin Donuts store. It was my first time and I ordered what Paul ordered, an egg and cheese sandwich. The girl heated packaged eggs in a microwave. Paul ate his sandwich, unperturbed, but I had reached my tipping point. I could sleep in a crappy hostel, I could spend two weeks in an underground garage to waiting for the van to sell, but I could not eat packaged eggs. I needed a job. It was that urgent.

I took my change and went to a phone booth. I opened the Yellow Pages phone directory and looked for M, MO, Modeling agencies. There were only three listed, which would simplify things. Paul was smoking outside, both intrigued by what they would say and annoyingly indifferent to my fate. I dialed the first number. A woman answered. Before I could get an appointment, I first had to send some pictures. I wrote down the information she gave me. Paul tapped on the door. "What did she say?"

"She asked if I had any modeling experience."

"Did you say yes?"

"No, I don't have any."

"If you want this, you're going to have to make something up."

I was not comfortable with lying but Paul was right. How would they know it wasn't true? I had nothing to lose. I dialed the next number and a girl with more enthusiasm picked up. I told her the little lie I had rehearsed. "When can you come over?" she asked. "Is Monday good?" It was in four days. Monday was perfect. Any day was. I didn't bother calling the last agency on the list.

Paul left on the Saturday night that followed my call to the agency. He had signed up for a trip up further north and said he'd be back in a week or so, until I figured out what I wanted to do about modeling. We each bought a mobile phone. This was the first time that we hadn't made any plans together. No maps had been spread out on the floor and no dreams had been shared and cheered for.

I moved to Kiwi Lodge, a cheaper place in town with dorm rooms of seven. I got my lunch from a lady down the road who sold street meat for $1.50 and when I went to the supermarket, I counted every penny I had in my purse before heading to the cash register. When a homeless man asked me for money outside, all I could offer him was a rollie. He was happy though and I lit one up for myself. My parents had sent me some money, but I had to stretch it, for an indefinite time and I had to pay Paul back for the repair on the van. But I didn't mind being cautious because I finally felt I had some control over my spending without Paul around. I met two English guys at the bar at Kiwi Lodge the night Paul left. They offered me two rounds of beer and paid for each game of pool. Things were looking brighter.

On Monday morning, I met with the modeling agency. I was wearing my best outfit: a sky-blue tank top stained with sweat marks under my armpits and a navy skirt cut just above the knee, washed out by the sun. Audrey met me at the top of a black metallic staircase. I liked her style; pointy boots, oversized shirt, leggings and rock and roll hair cut. Five large desks, arranged in a circle occupied the center of the agency. Three women, who were working the phones, glanced up at me and waved hello.

I followed Audrey to a private little room. She explained how everything worked; the agency would call me with castings, auditions for jobs, or go-sees, where you go and see a client and hopefully they remember you when you have a casting. Then she took some Polaroids of me, and then, very matter of factly, she got out a tape measure and wrapping her arms around my bottom, my waist and my breasts, she took my measurements. I was speechless. I gave her my cell phone number and a copy of my visa. The more Audrey spoke, the more excited I became. It sounded too good to be true and I worried that I didn't understand everything correctly.

"You have a strong face," she said. I didn't know what that meant. She reassured me saying that it was a good thing. "There's a hair show next week. I think you'd be really good for that. Let me talk to them and I'll call you afterwards, ok?" Where was the catch? "The job doesn't pay, but in exchange you'll get some pictures, which is what we need to get you started." If this was the catch, I was ok with it.

A white light creases the purple blue pastel sky to its heart in horizontal strokes over the Hudson River. I follow the veins of the sky on my bike. I'm going faster on my way back downtown. I feel the same urgency I felt in New Zealand to change something about my life—not my whole life again, but something. If happiness were an animal, it'd be a bird. Only when it is free can we follow its trail. The water, opaque and greenish turns a dark blue. In my mind, the flowers on my left smell like hay, the trees like roses and the seeds underneath my wheel, a forest. Roots, stems, and ears: life's carousel. All one. It feels great to be alive. The weather is *exquisite*–it would rhyme nicely with *squeeze* it. I feel high, like a battery fully charged.

I've enrolled in an acting class that starts in two weeks. I haven't told Andrew. I'm nervous, but ready for a new adventure–the unknown. I can see myself closing my eyes at the back of a motorbike with Paul. I'm in the driver's seat now. It's warm out and the gentle breeze rolls across my neck like silk chiffon. Winter is thawing, the promise of spring is in the air and I feel a little closer to myself again.

Mike lights a cigarette outside the restaurant where I met them inside for coffee, and offers me one. I decline. "You quit?"

"Yes, she did," Andrew says. He smiles proudly at me while I unlock my bike, and Mike disappears in a trail of smoke. "Put your bike in the trunk," Andrew says, pointing at his car parked on the other side of the street. "I thought you'd be tired."

I'm not. "We're so close, I'll ride back."

He stands motionless, his arms by his side. "I'm trying, Coline."

I feel guilty. "I'm sorry." I let him fold my bike and load it in the trunk.

We're already home when I realize I've forgotten my scarf in the restaurant. Andrew calls the place.

"I'm sorry, babe–they couldn't find it."

I call the restaurant myself to give a better description of my scarf. They're checking again. They come back on the line, apologizing. It's not there.

"We'll get you another scarf," Andrew says absently, as he types a message on his phone.

I don't want another scarf. I want the scarf I found in Thailand. It's the scarf that reminds me of all the goodness in the world, the scarf that means that anything is possible.

"I'm done with this," I say.

He puts his phone down. "What?"

"Us."

Andrew looks me straight in the eyes. "Where is this coming from? I love you, you love me and that's all that matters. As long as there's love, we can make anything work. That's what you said, remember?"

That's what I used to believe.

He dries a tear on my cheek. "You still love me, right?" Andrew asks. I sob and we embrace.

"I've got a job in Mexico next week. Maybe it'll be good for us to have some time apart, to think about what we want."

"I don't need you to go away on a trip to know what I want. I want you, babe. It's very simple."

Chapter 23

I meet up with Sarah at a bar in the West Village, where some friends of hers are playing in a folk-psyche-rock band. I run my fingers over the smooth jade pendant around my neck–a gift from a girl I met in New Zealand. The piece twists at the top, interlacing two threads and represents a sweet potato–a symbol of friendship. The band takes a break and Sarah introduces me to her friends. I find the singer-guitarist's scruffy beard, deep voice and soft smiling eyes very attractive. We chat before he returns to the stage.

Sarah has an early photo-shoot tomorrow and I still have to pack for my morning flight to Tulum. We raise our hand to say good-bye to her friends, and leave the bar under an explosion of blossoms–New York is at its most picture-perfect in April when the trees are flowering. On our way to the subway, we pass the studio where I enrolled for a class, and stop in front of a small brownstone. Sarah points at a window.

"See the sign there? You should take the number down."

"It's probably too expensive," I say.

"You never know."

I hesitate and take the phone number down on my phone. I feel like a little girl who just put her tooth under the pillow.

I was almost back to Kiwi Lodge when Audrey called on my mobile. "You're in for the hair show," she announced. "You got yourself an agent!" A fire crackled inside of me. I couldn't speak or move. I had just walked in the agency and already had a (non-paid) job! A car honked at me and I smiled, giddy and euphoric.

A few days later, I found myself standing at the same spot Paul and I had been on our first morning in Auckland. The tires attached to the dock screeched as men helped anchor a boat a few feet away from me. A briny smell of the harbor wafted over me, making all oceans one in my mind. I closed my eyes and thought of the Thames and of the beaches of Normandy. I missed my country. I missed speaking and hearing my language, the creamy and doughy patisseries, Mum's sweet smell and recognizing people on TV. I also missed the land where I had fallen in love with Paul, the school I had started my teaching career at and Paul's parents who felt like a second family, always inviting me for Sunday Roast. Someone coughed and the memories escaped, evaporated over the harbor. I had nothing in New Zealand: no money, no friends or family, but I liked this country. It held promises of positive changes.

Passengers got off the boat, unceremoniously. Auckland already no longer seemed unfamiliar—the city had a European feel to it. I had come to check the departure time for Waiheke Island so I too could go away on a trip. Paul now was in the land of geysers and I didn't know when I'd see him next.

I had arrived early at the salon the morning before to have my hair styled and make up done for the show. The hairdresser's friend applied a lot of blush and eye shadow on my face and gave me a silver tank top to wear, tucked in a black mini skirt with high heels. It was strange to transform from a girl to a woman. I barely recognized myself and I felt sexy for the first time in months, maybe ever. One day I was backpacking, and the next I was standing on a small pedestal next to seven other girls, while a panel of judges deliberated over who looked best. It was surreal.

A seagull played in the sky. I followed its loops, dives and arrow straight lines over the distant Waitemata harbor. A ferry pulled in. My phone rang. It was Paul calling to tell me he was not coming back to Auckland.

"Pack your bag and come!" he said.

I couldn't. The agency had already given me some appointments.

"Who gives a shit about those people? Just tell them to fuck off! She's just trying to put some guilt on you." I did not remember Paul ever cursing so much. "What about me, then? What about us?" A vertiginous pit cracked open in my stomach.

The ferry blew its horn and slowly pulled away from the dock. I tried to catch my breath and slow my racing pulse. I thought of the night Paul and I had decided to go traveling together, and how loved I felt. During our trip in Australia, I thought he had stopped and now, all of a sudden, he wanted me by his side. It was very confusing.

I was choosing a world of strangers over him. The ring he had bought me in Thailand, still hugging my finger, had made me feel we were engaged and committed to each other. One of us, or perhaps both of us, was breaking the bond. I couldn't bring myself to put my phone down.

The ferry's horn sounded again, the boat a shiny dot on the horizon, a dot telling me to be patient.

I remained on the cold bench for a little more, until it seized me: I may never see Paul again.

Chapter 24

I sign up on the casting call sheet by the door and take a seat amongst the small crowd of models along the corridor. I switch shoes and take out my ponytail–the job is for a hair color product. I don't mind the wait: I have work to do.

Without even looking up, I recognize Sarah's fragrance, tangy and sultry. We hug, she takes her coat off, signs up, and comes back to sit next to me. This is a big job that casts girls with every hair color.

"You're so tan," she says. "When did you get back?"

"Two days ago." Mexico already seems far away, as if there had been no break in between the disagreements I've been having with Andrew.

She picks up my book and reads the cover. "And you already have a monologue to prepare?"

The semester started yesterday. Even though I was a little tired from my trip and the long days of shooting, I couldn't miss it. "I was really scared before I walked in; I thought they'd all know more than me, but most of us are complete beginners. The teacher was great, really fun, and super patient. It felt like I was playing, like when we're kids and do role-playing." Sarah smiles over my enthusiasm and leafs through my book. "She gave us some monologues to choose from and then we talked a bit about each character."

"Which one did you chose?" Sarah asks.

"I haven't decided yet." I point at one monologue. "This one is called *Cigarettes and Chocolate*. It's about a girl who decides one day to stop speaking."

She laughs. "Why?"

A girl exits the casting studio and another one walks in, portfolio under her arm.

"Because she's tired of the useless conversations she's been having." I can feel my throat tighten. It sounds familiar. All those arguments with Andrew have only led to more disappointments.

"Ok. What's the next one about?"

"It's called *The Perfectionist*." I read aloud. *"I will never be perfect, no matter how hard I try."* All those efforts I made to try and fit into Andrew's world. All the efforts he recently made, but that came too late. And all the efforts I made to try and impress Dad, so I could still be worthy even as I was modeling. *"Sometimes I just want to end it all."* I can't read anymore.

"Maybe you should choose that one," she says. I look up and try to steady my breath. "It seems to resonate with you."

The casting director's assistant walks out, call sheet in hand. "Coline," she says, "you're up next."

I have to slip back into my model's role: I comb my hair with my fingers, and take a full deep breath in to relax my face and shoulders. I hand a comp card to the assistant and make sure my bra straps are tucked underneath my tank top. Sarah wishes me luck and I think of words like "yummy" and "fresh" as I walk into the room.

Central Park is in bloom. I lock my bike and settle down on a patch of grass by the pond to work on my monologue.

"Did you know that when I go to the grocery store, I spend twenty minutes trying to pick the perfect tomatoes for you? I spend twenty minutes on your stupid tomatoes! Perfection! That's what it's all about, isn't it? Well I give up."

I put my book down, lie on my back and stare at the dancing leaves in the uptown sky. In a couple of weeks the cherry trees will have covered the streets and alleys of New York City with pink cotton candy. I would not want to live anywhere else, with or without Andrew. Yesterday, I called about the apartment I saw with Sarah—it's free next month if I want it. The owner said I have to decide fast. I haven't even looked at other places. I lay my hands flat on the grass, palms facing down. Perched on branches high above, birds are chatting. What kind of stories are they telling each other?

I pick up the book my teacher told us to study. It falls open to a particular page. "It is only when an actor feels that his inner and outer life on the stage is flowing naturally and normally, in the circumstances that surround him, that the deeper sources of his subconscious gently open."

I rest, meditate on this and drift off to memories of the new life that was beginning for me in New Zealand.

Two cappuccinos sat steaming in front of us. Lisa, the owner of Bedford Square agency, had invited me for coffee on the terrace in the bright morning sun. A dark brown shawl in brushed silk hung gracefully over her shoulders, and a small pair of pearl earrings framed her beautiful face that bore very little make up. I would have been intimidated, but her smile was warm and the freckles on her cheekbones, golden.

"We got the pictures back from your test," she said. She pulled the photographs out of her handbag. "And we're quite excited about them…" I felt embarrassed—there were so many pictures of me. "I see the potential in you," Lisa said. She spoke in a slow, but firm voice. She was smiling, but not joking. "I think you should give it a try. A real try." I hugged my coffee cup between my palms and blew on it to cool it off. "Audrey told me about your financial situation: I'd like to help you." I was ready to refuse her help, but waited before reacting. "I'd like to offer you a place to stay here at the models' apartment."

"I can't afford it," I said.

"For free, Coline. You wouldn't have to pay me. Not until you start making money."

I was dreaming. There was a fairy sitting right in front of me, ready to tap her magic wand over my head, and I hesitated. This was not how I had been raised. Where I came from, we had to act with reason and realism.

She held her hand out. "Do we have a deal?"

I wanted to say yes with both my head and my heart. If I were meant to be with Paul, then we'd find a way to be together. "Yes," I said. We shook hands, and then I leapt up and gave her a hug.

I packed my bag at the hostel and moved in the model's apartment that same day.

Morgan arrived from America a month later. We became friends the moment Lisa introduced us to each other. She was a smart, kind, down-to-earth girl, who just happened to look gorgeous. She suggested that we go for sushi in town one night. I had never had sushi before. I didn't know if I could afford it—none of the jobs I had done had paid yet, but on the next day I was going to shoot my first television commercial, and this called for a celebration, Morgan said. We sat in a corner booth and when the waiter brought our platter of rolls Morgan showed me how to carefully mix wasabi into the soy sauce. Too much of it would make me cry, she said. I had learned my lesson in Thailand with Fred and Ana and mixed only a dab of wasabi in my little bowl—that was enough for me.

In between bites she said, "You've got to treat this job like a business." I had yet to decide if I would go back to France to enter the teaching school in September or back to England, which now seemed very unlikely–I hadn't had any news from Paul since a text message well over a month before, saying hi, nothing more. Meanwhile, I wanted to learn everything I could about my new job. "You're the only one who's gonna have your best interest at heart." Morgan sounded like a woman from Wall Street, with a language even more foreign than some of the terms I'd come across in the fashion world, "edgy" being one of them. I first had to open a "high yield saving account" and a "401K", or any French version for a retirement plan. A modeling career was short so you had to be smart, she said. This was a lot to think about while concentrating on eating sushi. I squeezed a raw piece of salmon in between my chopsticks and lost my rice to the soy sauce.

"When you come visit me in New York, I'll take you to a restaurant that makes really good sushi in the Lower East Side."

New York was the last destination on my round-the-world ticket. I wasn't ready to go back to Europe. I still hoped to see Paul before leaving New Zealand.

Wrapped in a towel, on the edge of the bed, my phone rang. Morgan was in the shower. It was Friday night and the agency was closed. It was Paul calling. My heart pounded against my ribs.

"Hey. How are you doing?" he started.

The first thing I noticed was that there was no "sweetheart" at the end of the line. The connection was very poor. "I'm good." Words came out uneasily from either side of our trivial exchange. I tightened up my towel around my chest and asked: "Are you calling to break up with me?"

"I thought about it, about us, a lot. But I don't think we can work this out. I'm sorry." A demonic elevator dropped me down fifty floors in a split second. "This trip was like a test for us and—"

"But, Paul, those were special circumstances." Maybe he had met someone. "You can't judge the whole relationship from this trip alone."

"If we can't travel together, we probably can't live together."

Yes, he had probably met another girl. I would forgive him. "But what about learning from experience? Isn't it what people do? It could make us stronger—"

"Coline. This is not going to work out. It's over. I'm sorry, sweetheart."

"But I won't model all the time! This is just for now! To try and make money and…" I tried to stand up, but my knees felt wobbly and I sank to the floor.

"I have to go, I'm running out of credit. I'm sorry."

"What? No! This is rubbish. Why are you lying?"

"I'm not. I'm gonna lose you. I don't have any more credit."

"Wait! Paul! Paul!" Emptiness resonated in my ears, followed by a series of "bips". The iron elevator doors closed on me, crushing my rib cage.

Morgan walked into my room, a towel around her head. "What happened?" She knelt down on the floor next to me.

"He just called. It's over."

She threw her arms around me and I broke into a heavy stream of tears. I didn't want it to be over with Paul, but Morgan was right—we could not keep on dragging around the dead weight our relationship had become.

"What do you want to do," she asked when I calmed down.

I held on to what I knew. "We said we'd go out tonight."

She offered me a tissue. "We don't have to."

I dried my eyes and blew my nose. "Well, I can either stay here and cry for the rest of the night, or we can go out and get drunk."

The rain was beating hard against the windows the following day. I felt betrayed by Paul and I had kissed a guy in a bar. I was very drunk. I felt as if my heart were being sawed into pieces. Everything was finished; backpacking with Paul, our possible plans to move in together, teaching one day in London, and even going to the teaching school in France next year felt like an old dream. The life I had known no longer existed. It had been that way the moment we had flown off to Thailand, and even the moment we had decided to go backpacking, but only now did I fully understand my loss.

Hung over, curled up in bed, I picked up my notepad to draw my feelings.

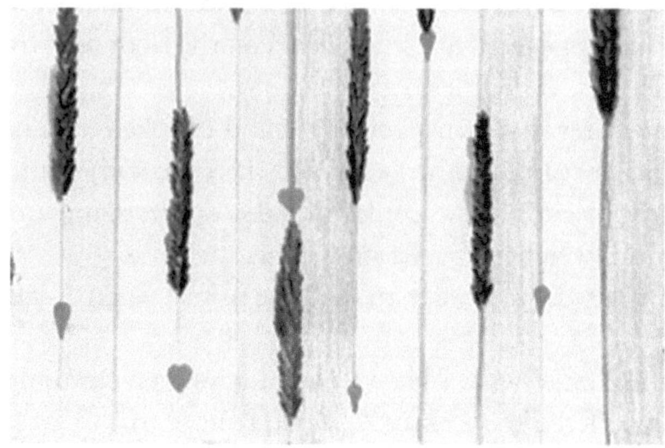

I named it "The mixing of events and emotions." It was about keeping on going and keeping on loving. I played with my ring Paul had given me. I never took it off, except for work. Now, with some difficulty, I removed it and put it in my vanity case. There was nothing to write. I couldn't form any sentences, but I had a direction to follow: I was going to give modeling a real try.

I picked up my paint and brushes, which I hadn't done in a long time. I didn't know what I was doing when I painted, but it made me feel better. Lighter.

I had to work with the shadows in my head. I had made a decision that would influence the rest of my life: after months of hesitation and anxiety, it came as a relief.

The chirping of the birds in the park bring me back gently to the present moment. I know what needs to happen. A similar sense of relief washes over me, along with a wave of sadness. I gather my books, call the owner to schedule a visit of the apartment and slowly ride back to Andrew's.

Chapter 25

The horrible part of a break-up is that you cannot be there for one another. It's over. This realization is as sudden as it is frightening. It's a pinch in the stomach that could make me vomit every time the word never comes to mind. Another person exiting my life. Another break-up. Another failure, I try not to think. Andrew got pushed over to the rank of 'exes', along with Paul. From Sarah's apartment in Brooklyn, the Manhattan skyscrapers are covered in a blue haze this morning. It feels late but the clock says it's not—we moved back an hour because of daylight saving last night.

At 9 a.m. yesterday I was in character study class. "Prepare consciously and then let your intuition enter your work," the teacher said. I picked up my text *The Perfectionist*. I had written the phonetics of some words in the margin, marked the separation of ideas and jotted down some specifics to have in mind. I wanted to be open to different responses, but anger was the first one that came through my actions. Every word out of me boiled with emotion. Each tomato became redder and fuller to the point of bursting open. The text did not matter, the subtext did. When I stopped, a calm and empty silence filled the room. I went back to my seat and knew my love for Andrew was gone.

I felt I was not being my true self with him. I had wanted to be a perfect girlfriend, just like I had wanted to be a perfect teacher, backpacker, and model. My frustrations with myself made me resentful towards Paul first, and now Andrew.

I packed a small bag to go stay at Sarah's for a few days and waited for Andrew to come back from lunch with Mike and his wife. I could not eat anything. My stomach was shaking.

He came in and went straight to the bedroom to change into his running clothes. I asked him to come sit on the couch with me. His phone vibrated, sending waves from his pocket to the cushions. I did not know how to start, where to look and what to do with my hands. I pressed them in between my knees and stared down at them. I could feel his gaze on me, as straight and confident as usual.

"I'm not sure I still love you," I said, finally looking him in the eyes. I could not recognize my voice.

Another phone vibration shivered across the couch.

"Sounds like you've made up your mind," Andrew cut in. He stood up, clenched his jaw tight, picked up his phone and said to whomever it was that he'd call back in two minutes. He put his trainers on. "If you want to leave, leave now," he said to me. "Make it fast." Before I could say another word he was out the door. I stayed on the couch, inert, for a while. I had to be practical: I called Sarah. She said she could come over to help me pack, but I needed to do this on my own. My New York life fitted into three suitcases.

The car service I had called was downstairs. I unclasped the diamond pendant around my neck and placed it in one of my now old drawers. I stood by the front door for one last look and remembered the day I had closed the models' apartment door in New Zealand with only a bag on my back. It was time to leave.

My worldly belongings were crammed into a backpack that was jammed in an overhead luggage bin. A connection in L.A was taking me en route to New York to visit Morgan for a few days, before heading on to my final destination, Normandy. I kept snoozing, my head resting against the window. "There are no beginnings without ends," I wrote in my diary as the lights of Auckland grew smaller and smaller after take off "and no ends without beginnings."

In the car Lisa had arranged to take me to the airport, I opened the little box she'd given me. There was a heart made of chocolate.

The air was dry in the plane and my eyes were red. Clouds and clouds were falling over each other outside my window. The thought of going home, seeing all the people I knew and loved so much, filled me with light. It was the right decision. Staying in Auckland without Paul, even when I wasn't earning much money, had also been the right decision for me. Trusting that voice had been the hardest challenge of my backpacking year, but also the most rewarding one—I felt stronger and more peaceful than ever before.

How things can happen so quickly, how so much can happen in such a short time is overwhelming. When you break-up, you know it's just a break-up. You know it happens to everybody and that most likely you will get over it with time. Yet, it is so excruciatingly painful, it seems no one can understand. It's a loss only you can mourn. That's why I haven't told Manu or other friends yet.

In Sarah's two-bedroom apartment on the thirtieth floor of a brand-new building, I begin a new cycle, one without Andrew. Four large windows rise up to the high ceiling of the living room, facing west. Only yesterday, I was looking east in Andrew's apartment: a big change of direction in a day. Now, a river flows between us.

The front door opens. Sarah—an angel in disguise—is back from her job.

"How are you feeling, Hon?"

"Comme-ci, comme-ca."

She drops her handbag in the living room and steps into the kitchen. Her long ebony hair falls to the side as she leans over the wine fridge. One glance at Sarah's golden hazelnut eyes shaped like two perfect almonds and it's easy to understand why at only twenty-eight she already owns her place.

"I got an email from him saying 'I told you not to waste my time.' Charming, no?" This is not like Andrew to be so mean. I collapse on her couch.

"He probably just said that to hurt you." She walks in with two full glasses of Chardonnay and sits down next to me. Her presence alone is comforting. "Take this time to focus on yourself. I was a mess after my break-up with Tyler last year. I went on a silent retreat after that. It was very challenging, to say the least, but I can say now that it's the best thing I've ever done for myself."

Here on Sarah's couch, clutching a pillow to my stomach, I feel pain. Is this just my ego? I am split between a sensation of peace and devastation. It's always the same wounds of insecurity that keep me away from my next goal. If I could follow my guts, despite all my fears and create a better life for myself in New Zealand, I should be able to do it again. The very worst of what I feared had happened; I had run out of money and my boyfriend had left me. Yet, or perhaps because of this, I discovered strengths I never knew I had.

I open my laptop and study the website my acting coach recommended. There's a weekend workshop coming up. Without thinking twice, I click on the "register" button.

Chapter 26

Sally, the teacher, gathers our small group of nine to the center of the room. It's the first morning of the workshop and quietly, this group of strangers form "the circle of trust." We hold hands to feel our energy as a group and let them hang by our sides. "Let's warm up our bodies. They are necessary instruments for any performance." We execute some shaking and vibrational exercises to liberate us from our body weight and consciousness. When we lie down, I feel heavy and relaxed. Sally suggests that we place our hands on each side of our rib cage to feel our breath going deep inside and outside of ourselves. My chest loosens up even more. The breath: such a simple and essential act and yet, so often forgotten.

"Now, I want you to visualize a room, somewhere familiar, like the first bedroom that you can remember."

The walls of my childhood were pastel pink with blue trees. There was a long windowsill I used to climb to watch passers-by, hurrying in the rain or chatting in the sun. I would get down and stare at my collection of small perfume bottles. When I didn't remember a smell, I'd open the bottle and breathe it in long enough to be able to recognize it in the streets if a woman would wear it. When my homework was done I would put on a CD and sing. I knew every word of every song of Les Innocents, the sad and happy ones. I would lie on my bed, look up at the ceiling and re-imagine the space; I could escape the cumbersome furniture that was the desk, the bed and the dresser, and feel light and free, up in the ceiling.

I'm moving into my apartment next week. I've never really lived by myself before. Loneliness is what scares me the most and paradoxically, being alone is what I need the most. The solitude I feel in the bedroom Sally asked us to revisit is peaceful. In my new place, I'll be able to decorate and paint the walls in the colors that I want, listen to my French music as loud and as often as I like, scatter my acting books on the floor, and burn up the perfumed candles of my choice.

"Henry, look for the specifics," the teacher says after lunch break. "What makes him who he is and not someone else?" Sally reminds me of Edith Piaf: a small woman with the energy of a giant. "Remember, it's by finding the specifics that we touch the general. There is a human condition common to all of us." I repeat this in silence. When I started modeling, I learned a new language. There's nothing different here.

Henry takes the time he needs to compose what is missing in his character and starts his scene over. As he opens the door again on set, I can tell the difference. I believe him. Whatever prompt he found worked. "There! You were living in the moment," Sally exclaims. The art of mimicking reality has a lot to teach to living fully. "Explore, take your time to take people in with you, have a strong objective, an intention, follow your instincts, be coherent, commit..." All of these sound like the Gospel to me.

On Sunday, the workshop starts with a voice class led by a different coach.

"Kick!" he says.

I throw my fist in the air and kick with my right foot. "Ha!" I shout.

"Let me hear it, Coline!"

I lash out a punchier sidekick and a growl comes out from my gut.

"Good!" he says. "You're finding your voice."

I am learning that I have a voice, that it lives in my stomach and not in my throat, and that I just need to breathe from down there to make it travel up to be heard. Through this vocal exploration, many emotional doors have opened. During an exercise yesterday, where we had to pull our tongue out as far as we could, lying on our back, I broke down in spasms. I wanted to excuse myself, but when Sally saw me looking for an exit, she encouraged me to continue the work.

"The throat is a very powerful place where we hide a lot of emotions," she said. "That's why we work with the whole body, because every part is connected."

I listened to my feelings, connected within, felt the mascara smudging on the side of my eyes, the soft and warm tears rolling down my neck and felt it all without judging it. Visualizing, meditating and acting are not about going far, but deep within. It is the door to our sky and the bottom of our ocean.

PART III

It is not easy to find happiness in ourselves, and it is not possible to find it elsewhere.
    —Melody Beattie, quoting Agnes Repplier.

Chapter 27

The truck should be here any minute now to unload the new furniture I ordered. The first and only thing I was able to hang was a hook for my bike in the closet. Andrew had left it in the lobby with the doorman like I asked him to. The plant he had offered me was there too—he had given it away to the doorman in the lobby, where it had a better chance to survive than in his apartment. I rode my bike over to the West Side Highway and stopped at a café on Christopher Street to get a frozen chocolate. I pushed my bike to the lawn on the small pier and scribbled a poem while sipping on my drink.

Enlightened and heightened
I stare at the world like I stare at myself
With gratitude and excitement
Manhattan
Inspires me in spite of me
The motion of my mind
Calm my heart, wave and weave
Peace in my own water
I surrender
Mother

Holy water
Manhattan
In your traffic, I repose
Pause and pause, body and soul
My body to my soul
Sole multiplicity
Multiple-city
Holy number
Manhattan
Complex city
Complicity

My new apartment overlooks a burgeoning tree and a cobblestone street. A squirrel was climbing the magnolia when the broker first showed it to me. I had not even broken up with Andrew yet. The second time I went to see it, I stood by the window, deciding if I should commit or not to this expensive rent and begged for a sign. While the broker was on the phone, the squirrel shook its tail, his way of saying hello, I thought. I had to go with my gut. Always.

The place will look bigger once the furniture is in and soon it will feel like home. What is *home* anyway? Is it a place with four walls and a ceiling, a place where you put the paintings and other knick-knacks you have been collecting? I open the window of my soon-to-be living room to let the smell of fresh paint disperse. The wind shuffles through the new leaves. A whiff of grilled meat tickles my nostrils from outside, maybe pork ribs. I'm hungry. "When aren't you?" Sarah would say. She knows me well by now. Moving in means that this is the end of my stay at Sarah's and tonight is our last dinner as roommates.

The delivery truck is on time. I spend the rest of the morning arranging furniture and emptying boxes and suitcases. I can't do it all in a day and it's a good thing; I need to take my time to select what I really want in my home. I put my favorite books on the coffee table and leave the others in the box. My vintage perfume bottles are the first items to go in the bathroom. Sarah calls to offer help but I am happy to be alone. I meet up with her on the farmers market in McCarren Park later in the afternoon. We get an organic chicken, rosemary, lemons, onions and garlic, eggs and chocolate.

A few hours and a bottle of Gavi later, the bird calls from the oven while the mousse solidifies in the fridge.

"I think it'll be great for you to be on your own, hon."

I grab the big knife and pause. "I agree." I cut the two legs off and place one on each plate. We switch to a bottle of Pinot Noir. "Acting is changing my life, you know."

She laughs. I'm a little tipsy. "How was class last night?"

"The teacher taught us about Meisner. We learned a new acting technique of talking and listening, where we had to work on an impulse from the other person and from what we were feeling." Words didn't matter in the exercise. "We repeated the same phrase over and over again, but each time we delivered the line, it landed in a different way." I put my fork down to demonstrate how the exercise went.

"Hu, interesting." Sarah pours more wine in the glasses.

"You know what else is interesting—by the way, this chicken is delicious—"

"Thank you."

"—it made me think about Andrew. And Paul, too. If I had *listened* to them. Like *really* listened. For instance, Paul would say he needed *space*, but he did not mean a *physical* space. And Andrew, if I had carefully listened to him, maybe I would have seen how he really cared about me. Oh, I don't know."

"Hon, you can't put all the blame on yourself for past relationships."

"I know. But I blamed *them* for the way I felt, lonely and uncared for. I should have taken care of myself instead of expected them to take care of me."

She nods.

I raise my glass. "To you," I say. "I don't know what I would have done without you."

"And to Rambo!"

"Rimbaud," I correct.

I recently volunteered for an animal shelter and fell in love with a kitten, grey with black stripes. It's still a baby and needs to stay at the shelter for another couple of weeks, but I filled out the adoption papers. I named him after one of my favorite French poets.

I carry the mousse to the table and we fill our bowl with unction and sweetness.

Chapter 28

Meandering along a mountain road in the Engadine valley of Switzerland, a shaft of sunlight keeps appearing and disappearing through the dark branches, momentarily blinding the crew and me in this very early morning. We are driving up to the first shooting location of the day. The light shining through the pine trees is subdued, which pleases the photographer. He wants to shoot as much as possible before the sun rises too high. There is still half an hour-drive to the little chalet. I stare through the car window at the conifers standing tall, as if to protect their alpine habitat, including even the tiniest little flowers in the soft shades of blue, white and pink on the side of the road. Branches hefty with snow fold back onto the forest, withdrawing from the people, and muffle the crispy sound of the tires on the road.

I recall a family trip to the Alps one Christmas and the sinuous road winding uphill. My ears were aching. "Pinch your nose," Manu said, "and blow." They would not pop. The drive was long and we had left home in the middle of the night to avoid traffic. Because I was the youngest and smallest one, I slept on the floor of the car, behind the front seats.

We pull off at a chalet overlooking a mirror lake—the mountains seem crystallized in its water. We all help to unload the photographic equipment inside. The lady of the house has prepared breakfast for us, a very hearty breakfast. I warm up just by the smell of it. I grab a bowl and serve myself generously from the pan of oatmeal, adding a spoonful of dried fruits and nuts.

Mum would heat up some baked beans in a pan and sausages in another. "Fast and filling," she would say. Manu and I had to swallow two nasty brown vitamin pills before eating our lunch. I can still taste their metallic tang. While we did the dishes, Dad sipped his coffee in the sun on the terrace, reading the papers. His lips were white from the SPF lip balm we all wore on a string around our neck. I think of the clothes we were wearing: a pink jacket for Manu, a green one for me, red for Mum, navy blue for Dad, ski pants that clipped on the shoulders, layers of turtle-necks and sweaters underneath. It makes me smile now to be modeling designer ski suits, the kind I could only ever dream of wearing when I was a kid.

On that Christmas Eve, at exactly midnight, I unwrapped a jewelry box. It was made of wood, varnished on the outside and lined with red velvet: there were lots of little drawers. Manu had made me a pearl bracelet and that was the first thing I placed in the box.

Christina calls me over to get started with the makeup. "Close your eyes," she says. I feel the delicious warmth of the sun all over my face through the window in front of me. It's easy to focus on the lows in my job and forget how fortunate I am to be modeling, traveling and meeting so many kind and creative people. I miss my family, but I know our love for each other transcends physical boundaries. I don't need to be in France to feel close to them. In New Zealand, I felt far away from everyone because I felt far away from myself–I didn't know who I was, or what I wanted.

I was visiting Waiheke Island, when Audrey called to send me to a casting in town–a cover for a bridal magazine. I didn't have time to go to the models' apartment to change and met with the client in zip-off trousers and walking boots. Butterflies were fluttering their wings in my stomach. I had booked my first job.

"Don't move," the makeup artist said. I had arrived early at the photo studio, and after briefly being introduced to the team, was sitting in front of a mirror framed with light bulbs. I held my breath as the makeup artist curled my eyelashes with a scary metal tool that looked like it could inflict serious harm. She then held my eyelids open with her index finger and applied a thick coat of mascara. I pretended I was having a staring contest with Manu. I didn't blink once.

A few more days in Switzerland and I'll be with Manu. She took a day off to celebrate my birthday.

Little girls, we would return our empty glasses at the kitchen table and check the serial numbers engraved at the bottom: it would tell us how old we were going to be that day–that was the game.

"Twenty-eight," Manu said one morning after drinking her orange juice. "I'm twenty-eight! I beat you."

"You're *old*," I said with a grimace.

Well, here we are. I'll be twenty-eight next week.

I sometimes wonder about the place and importance memories have. Andrew and I were together for almost three years and one day we weren't anymore. Was he right? Was our relationship a waste of time?

Memories create a space that allows me to select what I want to keep in my jewelry box. Acting is teaching me how to open the drawer corresponding to the emotion I am looking for, and transform it into creative energy. The good times I shared with Andrew—my first time ice-skating with him in the park, the carriage ride that followed and the mountain of gifts he had brought for his family the one Christmas we spent together—can make me smile now.

Happiness is the only riches of value. It is my job to create happy moments for myself. I want to pick up some paint and brushes again, go to museums, explore, wherever I find myself. Why did I stop doing this? It was one of the things that made me the most joyful when I was backpacking.

I called Morgan the other day. (She moved to Lake Tahoe soon after I moved to New York.) It was as if all those months of silence had never existed. We talked as if we'd last spoken yesterday, reminiscing about New Zealand; the crêpes we made for the girls at the agency, her teaching me how to walk the runway, our glacier climb in Queenstown...

"Let's go backpacking," Morgan announced at breakfast one morning. Work was slow and our bookers said that the next two weeks were going to be worse. It was a good time to travel. "I printed out some maps," she said over her scrambled eggs, and laid them down on the table. Her enthusiasm was waking me up from my mini-modeling coma. I opened my guidebook and together we drew the first leg of the journey to Rotorua. My travel bug had returned and meeting Morgan seemed like a dream come true. Several times along the journey with Paul had I envied girlfriends going on an adventure together.

With thrills and a few shivers of apprehension, we heaved our bags onto our backs. We must have looked funny—two models going backpacking. We traveled by car, ferry, and magic bus, making our way down to the south island. It was in Queenstown that we saw people paragliding.

"How osome," I said.

Morgan laughed. "You mean *awe*some."

I was in *awe*, yes, but I couldn't afford the jump. I was finally making a little money modeling, but I had a rent and debts to pay back. Morgan got confirmed for a last minute job in Auckland and flew back before me. I stayed in Wakatipu Lake and watched the ducks, diving their heads, stretching their necks, shaking their bums and doing it all over again. In the distance, paragliders brushed the horizon and my vision blurred with theirs, as if I too were soaring.

Chapter 29

I follow the Boulevard St Germain, pass the Pont de la Concorde and arrive at the Musée de l'Orangerie. I have a few hours to spend in Paris before my flight back to New York this evening. Outside the museum, I melt under Rodin's sculptural hands as if I were the one being enlaced, touched, kissed with all this love and passion and tenderness that read in every movement he molded in his sculptures. Inside the two oval rooms, built especially to host the eight murals by Monet under direct sunlight, the Nymphéas capsize me. I alternately feel flowed with excitement and soothed by the peaceful state of each scene. I lose myself in the clouds reflected in the ponds and brought to life in romantic pastel hues of blue. I'm looking for a door that will let me into this world. I want to cross the bridge, touch the flowers and let their fragrance travel inside me. I take a seat on a bench in the middle of this whirl-winding room and remain into this far away place until a crowd of tourists jolts me from my reverie.

I walk down to a space dedicated to the collection of Paul Guillaume, a famous art dealer. The man's eclectic preferences strike me. The portraits by Chaim Soutine, an expressionist, are underlined by a comment from Paul Guillaume: "La mesure et la démence luttent et s'équilibrent," – "Order and excess struggle and balance." Dissymmetrical and classic forms, as well as violent and peaceful pieces seemed to have inspired the man.

In the plane, the phrase sinks inside me a little further. If order and disorder can live harmoniously in a piece of art, can it be the same in life? Is it all a question of balance—in the sky, in the heart?

When a moment is beautiful, it has a picture quality, as if our heart went *click* and took a moving photograph to materialize this special experience—a communion between nature and us, or between people. It's when two or several become one. Beauty has the power to take us from the position of mere witness to actor and the moment becomes present and alive because we are part of it. But it cannot exist if we don't care for it. A work of art is beautiful when it awakes something in us—an impression that moves us inside, giving birth to a feeling of harmony.

When I let fear paralyze me, I am no longer able to appreciate the beauty of my surroundings. The experience of *contrast* is essential to living—it can't all be perfect. Perhaps the reason why traveling broadens the mind is that the more we experience, the more contrast we can perceive, and the more we can appreciate life.

When Paul and I decided to drive through the desert in Australia, people told us that there was nothing to see there. "Nothing" does not exist. Feeling the vastness, trying to understand what we cannot see, cannot touch, where things end and start is something. I was on a quest, looking for what made me unique, and I've come to realize that we also are one and the same, thirsty for beauty, authenticity and connections. We are all different, but *same-same...*

Perhaps Soutine saw the beauty in those imperfections that make us human.

My own reflection teases me in the window. It is easier to find myself beautiful on the page of a magazine or catalogue, with makeup on, a flattering light, and the magic touch of a photo editing software, than *au naturel*. I stare at my image because I want to see that I'm beautiful without artifacts, that my true beauty lies inside of me, in my ability to integrate and harmonize the whole of me.

Chapter 30

A bright yellow leaf flies in through the open window of the restaurant and lands on the table between Sarah and me. A caress of cool autumn air follows and makes the hair on my forearms stand up. I don't mind the rain of the last few days; I am ready for a change of seasons and some snuggling time with Rimbaud.

"Is all your meat organic?" Sarah asks the waiter. A few signs by the register praise the quality of their kobe beef.

Assured that the meat is grass-fed with no antibiotics, we order two burgers with salad on the side. Sarah, her long ebony hair held up loose in a low ponytail over her leather jacket, responds quickly to a message on her phone while I turn mine to silent.

"I saw you last night on TV!" she says suddenly. I got a small part in a new series, a lucky number based more on my modeling quality than my acting skills.

"They cut off some of my lines. I knew that was to be expected, but still, it sucks."

"Shush! You looked great!"

I take a long look at the unusually goofy expression on her face. "How was your third date with Tom?" I ask.

She smiles and rolls her eyes up to the ceiling. "Good…" Someone closes the window. "What about you, hon? Any cutie in Switzerland? A handsome skiing instructor?"

"I don't really care for anyone right now."

"Not even my friend Matias? He asked about you…"

I look away for a second. "I've got a new male in my life now and he's very territorial!" Rimbaud has stolen my heart. "And I'm busy with my classes." I need time alone. I've accomplished so much in the last six months and I want to continue that way.

Sarah bites into her meat, red and juicy. I dig avidly into mine. "Come with me tonight," she says, in between bites. "Margo's throwing a party."

"I can't. I have a really big audition tomorrow morning."

Sarah wipes the corners of her mouth and fixes me with her arms crossed over the table. "I'm so proud of you."

A feeling of warm satisfaction envelops me. Sarah is smiling like I've never seen her before. "Let's get the check, Miss Love," I say, "or you'll be late for your casting."

We step outside, into the rays of sunshine that play with the clouds and warm up the brownstones in vivid hues of red. A rainbow of brown, bordeaux and orange leaves colors the cobblestone streets. It feels like only yesterday cherry blossom petals were falling down around us. Now large pots of bright orange chrysanthemums adorn the steps of the neighboring brownstones.

"See you Saturday!" she shouts.

"8am!" I shout back.

The wind swells and gently lifts up my skirt. I find a bench in the sun in front of a café and pull out my lines for my audition. Another gust of wind blows my hair over my face and sends a few golden leaves dancing off the ground.

A man opens the door and a whiff of hot chocolate flirts with the air. I concentrate on my pages, but there's no need to keep reading, I know my lines. What I need is to practice the different reactions I could have for the scene where I confront my cheating boyfriend. I could play being hurt and vindictive, unaffected and disdainful or I could be gentler. I'll see what feels best tomorrow.

Did I make the right choice? The girl who was struggling to decide between teaching and modeling, going home or staying in New York, has never left me completely. There are no more promises with acting than with modeling, but I don't feel the same way I used to. I'll probably always be scared, but that's how I move towards new and exciting things in life.

The wind shuffles again from east to west and I almost lose my lines. It is time to go home. I shove my pages in my bag and get up. A drop of rain falls onto my forehead, and an unseen hand watercolors the sky in metallic blue. I like the humid smell of rain and how it touches my skin, timidly at first, confidently afterwards. One drop becomes two, then three, then more. It rolls and slides down my face like a caress.

Through the curtain of drizzling rain a face smiles at me across the street—Matias! Shall I stop and say hi? I hesitate. The picture of Rimbaud curled up on my couch forms in my head. I want to go home and continue practicing my scene. The silver rain makes me shiver and the sky growls over my head. I wave a slight salute to Matias and disappear at the next street corner.

A thick and bubbly envelope with a French stamp is waiting in my letterbox—a present from Manu. A neighbor walks out and holds the door open for me. I call for the elevator and as the door closes on me, I glance at myself in the hallway mirror; my hair is a mess, my leather sandals a ruin, but I don't care.

When I get home, I drop my handbag and the mail to the floor, and hang my jacket, heavy and soggy. Rimbaud greets me in the hallway, gliding in between my legs, begging for tender loving care. I squat down to scratch behind his ears and all the right places that make him purr. I strip off my wet clothes and change into a pair of comfy sweatpants. I think of my character and wonder if she would react differently if she had met a guy as cute-looking as Matias. What I like about acting is that I get to play, even by myself. I make up stories like I used to do with my Barbies and Legos. New ideas and emotions spring up when I play my character, as if I were high, and when my scene is done, and I'm happy with where I went, I feel calm again, as if a wave had washed over me with new imagery and sensations, some fleeting, others more palpable.

I boil some water, pour it in my favorite cup, the one with the quote from Thoreau about living your dreams. I play my scene one more time with this improvised prop. The more I practice, the more prepared I'll be when I stand before strangers tomorrow.

I nestle with Rimbaud on the couch, beneath the windowsill. I could stroke him forever. The sunshine breaks through the clouds and glistens on the puddles outside. I look for a fluffy tail in the bush, but our friend is in hiding. I pick up Manu's envelope. It holds something hard and rectangular. I tear it open and laugh: she's sent me a Galak bar—an old brand of white chocolate that we used to devour when we were kids at my grandparents'. The

80's TV commercial was a cartoon with two children on a boat, making friends with a dolphin. When the Galak bar appeared on the screen, it was as if they had found gold and everyone looked so happy. She's attached a few photos we took the day we spent together for my birthday this summer, treetop trekking and zip-lining in the woods. We both look very flushed and happy.

"Did you think it was going to be easy?" Manu said when we got to the woods, where tall oak trees filtered the light of the day. We were standing in front of the most challenging obstacle: four jumps on logs wobbling in the air and a platform about fifty feet high. A harness cut into my shorts as if I had a big diaper.

"I thought we were going to play Tarzan and swing like monkeys," I said. I locked my carabiner to the line that the instructor called a *lifeline* and threw myself off the initial platform and missed the first log. It's not physical, it's mental, I told myself, as I twisted my way back onto the platform. I had to let go of my fear of falling. I could not fall–I had a lifeline. I tried again. I pressed my butt down, rocked back and forth on my knees for momentum, and jumped, letting out a cowboy scream. Manu was laughing. I had made her promised me a Galak bar if I succeeded.

My first impulse is to save the chocolate bar, but then I decide to get a bite of the memory. They haven't changed the recipe: it smells as sweet as I remember. I take a sip of tea and burn the tip of my tongue, which instantly melts the second piece of chocolate I take. Rimbaud sniffs my fingers with dislike and spins around on my lap. It tastes of milk and concentrated sugar. It tastes of old people, of Pépé's friends who would often stop by for coffee, and of Grandma's suction kisses. It's addictive–I could eat the whole bar.

There's one more photo in the envelope: a picture of us, little, picking dandelions in a field. Manu wrote something underneath: *You and I, blowing on the flowers of our future, making wishes. I hope yours come true.*

I can't help but shed a tear. I feel protected by a bubble of unconditional love. Manu taped a dried dandelion–our magical flower–next to her loving words. From the inside of the envelope, I collect the fallen seeds, place them in the center of my hand and spread my wishes around for success, both in acting and modeling, good health, strong friendships and love.

The sky turns navy blue. I spy our little friend's tail moving about in the tree. I turn my back to the window and take in my new home. The ficus tree, the bamboo shoots, the Moroccan wool rug, the orangey-pink wall I painted, and the framed photos of my parents and Manu visiting me one year make the place feel warm and cozy. A sense of peace and safety has now settled in. Finding a place to call home has been a full journey. It was as challenging to travel thousands of miles as to take a few deep breaths right where I was.

Home is the place where all those I love live, where all my passions lie, and my memories rest. The toothless old man I visited in Pie is still somewhere inside of me, even though I never did find my beloved scarf, and so are all the men I've loved and experiences I've had. A part of them will stay with me forever, so I never travel alone in the world. When I had a backpack I thought I needed to stay put in one place to be at home, but an address does not make for a home. I wouldn't be home much if it was just a physical place. Being in the present is something acting has taught me. I can feel at home in planes and airports, at my parents', abroad, or in my apartment. What matters is not the place I'm in, but the space that I create for myself inside my heart.

Chapter 31

The September sky is clear, save for a few wispy clouds out, and there is a light breeze. Sarah, Morgan, and I met up at eight this morning at the car rental place and drove out to New Jersey. We are going paragliding and I am first to try.

My instructor stands behind me on top of the hill. "Ready?" he asks. A few feet below, my friends scream encouraging words. I am a body in transformation, ready to take off and fly. Past sensations flash by me at the speed of the adrenaline running through my veins: the speedboat over the Mekong, the motorbike rides through the Vietnamese mountains, the balloon ascension in Australia, the phone call to the modeling agency, moving to New York, my first acting class... "Yes," I answer.

"Now!" the instructor yells. "Start running!"

I put one foot in front of the other as fast as I can—they're as heavy as two sand bags—it's like I'm treading water.

"Keep running," the instructor shouts. I squint my eyes in the effort and run even harder, blind to everything around. "OK, you can stop now."

When I reopen my eyes, we have left the ground. My feet are still paddling, as if I were a beheaded coq, running on nerve impulse. Morgan and Sarah's cheers linger in the distance. The air is light and the clouds that were cast about the sky twenty minutes ago have all dissipated. The half-moon shadow of the kite on the ground moves along with us. I am flying into the wind of the unknown, the infinite.

The wind of the unknown

Blowing into the wind of the unknown,
The sun attached to the tip of its spine,
The dandelion is glowing—a heart full of light.

Hello for now but tomorrow, goodnight.
The gold will mature at the head of the line
And the moon shine, far away, on its own.

Slowly, the lion peels the layers of its youth.
The weed is dense and the starry seeds balance—
Millions will fly and spread, searching for their truth.

Acknowledgements

This book has been a work of love and many fears. It has grown along with me for several years and I am thankful to every single person who has touched my life.

I feel unconditional gratitude for the constant support my friends and family have given me, both through the challenging times and when it called for celebration. Their loving presence has helped me follow the journey of self-discovery with peace and joy in my heart.

A deep thank you to Lisa Fugard, Claire Fricke, and Alexandria Berry for their precious patience and smart edits. They have transformed this book into the best version of itself.

I am also infinitely grateful to all the teachers and healers I have been fortunate to meet. In their own way, they have helped me see who I could become when I let go of my fear of the unknown. It is a beautiful place to embrace.

About the Author

Sandrine Marlier-Riquier was born and raised in small towns in France. After English studies in Normandy and Birmingham, U.K., she went on to assist French classes in Guernsey, C.I., followed by a gap-year traveling the world. While in New-Zealand, she switched direction and discovered the fashion world.

At 34, Sandrine is still modeling and traveling the world. This semi-autobiographical novel is Sandrine's first book. She currently lives in New York, has started a life coaching practice and is working on a children's book.